屈原楚辞英译

赵彦春 译·注

屈原（约公元前340—前278年） 绘画：李俊琪

上海大学出版社
Shanghai University Press

⊙ 赵彦春 译·注
Translated and Annotated by Yanchun Zhao

屈原
楚辞英译
Odes and Elegies by Yuan Qu
in English Rhyme
Approaching Hermes and Muses Reincarnate

序 | Foreword

读赵彦春教授《屈原楚辞英译》有感

赵彦春教授的《屈原楚辞英译》即将付梓，嘱予说几句话，乃得先睹为快。赵彦春教授已经翻译了很多中国古典诗词作品，他的翻译既照顾到翻译文本的信和达，也照顾到诗歌的雅意和诗意，这是很难做到的。

以前，许渊冲先生的英译文本曾是我最喜欢的；现在，赵彦春教授的英文译本也是我最喜欢的。中国古典诗歌讲究诗心、意境、格调、意象、音律、神韵、肌理、哲思，而这些内容在语言表达上都是非常微妙的。我曾经认为诗歌是不能翻译的，也是不能移植的。但是当我读了赵彦春教授的译文之后，我改变了自己的看法。赵彦春教授的译文语言清丽，格调高雅，诗歌的韵味十足。楚辞是非常高古的，今天我们读《离骚》《九歌》《九章》有很多地方都很难理解透彻，毕竟在时空上我们跟屈原是有距离的。尤其是诗中涉及大量的植物名称，而每一种植物名称都有隐喻意义和象征意义，在翻译成另外一种语言的时候，很难找到对应的植物。译者做了深入的研究，了解英文植物的隐喻意义和象征意义，十分出色地把它们翻译出来，真是难能可贵。

我们都知道，中国古典诗歌都是押韵的，而且是押尾韵，在翻译的过程中要保留它们的韵脚这是十分不容易的。汉语的单音节性决定了中国古典诗歌的押韵特点，在译本中还要保留这些韵律的特征，就要煞费苦心。有的翻译家在翻译中国古典诗歌的时候，会牺牲掉中国诗歌的韵律特征，转而追求诗歌的散文美。赵彦春教授力图保留诗歌原来的韵味，力求形神兼备，可谓匠心独运。

中国是一个诗歌大国，每一位诗人都有自己的个人风格和特色，或婉约或豪放，或"郊寒岛瘦"，各有千秋。在翻译中要照顾每个诗人的个性特点。屈原的诗歌有一种不屈不挠的精神和郁郁寡欢的气质。所以当一个人遇到不如意的事情时会想到"痛饮酒，读离骚"。这是诗歌当中的气脉。在屈原的诗里边，这些气脉由句末语气词来表达，在英文译本中译者把它们变成了句首感叹词。我认为这种处理很妙。英文没有句末语气词，只有感叹词，它们同样可以表达言者的情态意义。不知道英文读者是否会有"痛饮酒，读离骚"的阅读体验。

赵彦春教授是我的老朋友，近年来一直从事中国古代诗歌的翻译工作。他和他的团队非常勤奋，他翻译了《三字经》《诗经》《论语》《道德经》《庄子》《王维诗歌全集》《李白诗歌全集》《杜甫诗歌全集》以及三曹诗歌全集等中国古典诗词，也翻译过林徽因的现代诗歌《人间四月天》等。从这些翻译作品中可以看到翻译家的二次创作。更重要的是我们可以从他的文字中读到趣味、情怀和诗心。让我们期待这部屈原诗歌英译本的问世吧！

崔希亮 于京华朝暾堂
2022 年 2 月 1 日

Reading Yanchun Zhao's *Odes and Elegies by Yuan Qu in English Rhyme*

I'm asked to say a few words as Prof. Yanchun *Zhao's Odes and Elegies by Yuan Qu in English Rhyme* is coming out and I have the pleasure of being its first reader.

Professor Yanchun Zhao has translated many classic poems and his translations have not only the merits of faithfulness and expressiveness but also the capture of poetic elegance and significance, which is so hard to come by.

Professor Yuanchong Xu's English Translations were once my favorite; now, Professor Yanchun Zhao's English versions are my favorite as well. Chinese classic poetry is particular about poetic feeling, artistic conception, literary style, romantic charm, imagery, prosody, texture and philosophical cognition. I once denied the translatability or transplantability of poetry and now I'm converted, having read Professor Zhao's translations. His translations brim with beauty and elegance, a lingering appeal of poetic charm. Chu verse is cryptically old. Much of *Woebegone*, *Nine Songs* and *Nine Cantos* is too hard to have a good understanding of. We are distant from Yuan Qu in time and space after all. What is special is that a large number of plants appear in the poems and every plant carries a metaphorical or symbolic meaning and significance. It's often hard to find their equivalents in the target language. The translator made intensive research to explore their metaphoricity and symbolism and translated them into excellence. What a high-finesse manoeuvre!

As we all know, classic Chinese poems are all in rhyme, and in end rhyme in particular. It is very hard to retain the rhyme and one need take pains to retain it as well as the prosodic features because the monosyllabicity of Chinese determines the idiosyncrasy of rhyming of classic Chinese poetry. Some translators give up the prosody of Chinese poetry and pursue but the beauty of prose. Professor Yanchun Zhao endeavors to keep the poetic charm of the original, both in form and meaning. What a commendable act of exertion!

China is a great country of poetry and every poet has his own style or features, restrained grace or forthright pride, "the coolness of Jiao or the leanness of Dao", each having his own merits. Every poet's idiosyncrasy should be considered in translation. Yuan Qu's poetry has a strain of tenacity and sullenness, so when in unfavorable conditions, one will often "have an impassioned drink and read *Woebegone*", as is the mood channel of poetry. In Yuan Qu's poetry, such a mood channel is expressed with a modal particle at the end of a line. In these translations, this device is represented with an interjection at the beginning by analogy, as is a subtle deft treatment I think. English does not have modal particles except interjections which can also be used to express a speaker's modal meaning. I don't know whether an English reader has the same reading experience of "having an impassioned drink and reading *Woebegone*".

Professor Yanchun Zhao is my old friend. He has been working on some projects of Chinese classic poetry translation in recent years. He and his team are very industrious. He has translated *Three-word Primer*, *the Book of Songs*, *the Analects*, *the Word and the World*, *Sir Lush* and complete editions of poems by Wei Wang, Bai Li and Fu Du and complete editions of Three Cao's poems besides modern poetry by Phyllis Lin and so on. From such translations you can see a translator's re-creation. More importantly, from his words we can read his interest, feelings and poetic heart. Let us look forward to the coming out of Yuan Qu's poetry in English rhyme.

Xiliang Cui at Aurora Hall, Peking
Feb. 1, 2022

目录 Contents

Foreword 序 1

Woebegone 离骚 63

Nine Songs 九歌 63
- Great One, Our Lord East 东皇太一 64
- Lord in Clouds 云中君 68
- Lord of Xiang 湘君 71
- Lady of Xiang 湘夫人 77

Nine Cantos 九章 115
- O Remonstration 惜诵 116
- Crossing the River 涉江 130
- Thought Reeled Off 抽思 142
- Mourning Ying, the Capital 哀郢 154
- Thinking of Sand 怀沙 164
- The Beauty I Miss 思美人 176

礼魂 Soul of the Rite	113
国殇 The Death of the State	110
山鬼 Mountain Ghost	103
河伯 River God	99
东君 East Lord	94
少司命 Life God Junior	90
大司命 Life God Senior	84
惜往日 Missing the Bygone Day	188
橘颂 Ode to the Orange	200
悲回风 Mourning the Whirling Wind	206
天问 Asking the Sky	225
招魂 Evocation	293
渔父 The Fisherman	341
跋 Postscript	349

离骚

Woebegone

2

帝高阳之苗裔兮,

朕皇考曰伯庸。

O I'm a descendant from Lord High Sun,
And my late father was called Use One.

摄提贞于孟陬兮,

惟庚寅吾以降。

O in Prime Spring, Jupiter came to shine
O'er my birth on Tiger, a month fine.

离骚

---

*Lord High Sun: Plump Head, Zhuanxu if transliterated, Lord Yellow's grandson, named after the capital of his fief, High Sun, in today's Qi County, Henan Province. He reigned 78 years (2519 B.C.-2436 B.C.).
*Use One: Boyong if transliterated, the author's father. "Use" in the name and as a name is a code of an important philosophical concept of doing, performance, practice or utility in contrast with the ultimate ontological "Word" or "Being" while "One", a morpheme used in this first name, indicates his primogeniture as the first son.
*Prime Spring: the first moon according to Chinese calendar.
*Jupiter: the yearly star in Chinese astrology and astronomy, the fifth planet from the sun, around which it revolves about 12 (117/8) years at a mean distance of 483,000,000 miles. And Jupiter is a year because its orbit, close to the ecliptic, is divided into twelve parts, which represent 12 years, and accordingly one year is called one Jupiter year, Jupiter for short.
*Tiger: name of a lunar month according to Chinese calendar, approximately the period between Beginning of Spring (Lichun) and Stunned (Jingzhe).

3

皇览揆余初度兮，

肇锡余以嘉名：

O my sire observed the hour when came I
And gave me auspicious names thereby.

名余曰正则兮，

字余曰灵均。

O my formal address was Rule Right,
And my familiar one was Fair Sprite.

纷吾既有此内美兮，

又重之以修能。

O with inner beauty I was so well blessed,
And to raise my own worth I tried best.

---

*Rule Right: the appellation or formal address of our poet, Yuan Qu (cir. 345 B.C.-286 B.C.). According to *the Rites of Zhou*, a boy is given his formal name three months after his birth, used on formal or ceremonial occasions.
*Fair Sprite: our poet's style or familiar address. In ancient China, a boy was given his familiar name when he had grown up to manhood at the age of twenty, addressed by his relatives and friends for daily use.

4

扈江离与辟芷兮,

纫秋兰以为佩。

离骚

O selinea 'n angelica I don;
A eupatory sash I put on.

汨余若将不及兮,

恐年岁之不吾与。

O the tide I can't catch up with runs fast;
The time that does not wait for me flies past!

---

*selinea: an aromatic herb, an umbelliferous plant one to two feet tall, often knit into apparels or braided as pendants, or used as a vegetable or medicine.
*angelica: an odoriferous herb over four feet tall, blowing small white flowers in clusters in summer, usually used as a decoration for sashes or pendants in ancient China, its roots often candied as a confection.
*eupatory: an aromatic herb, growing by waterside, with purple stems, red at protuberant joints, four to five feet tall, with glossy leaves which are long, pointed at end and saw-toothed on edges, luxuriant in summer.

朝搴阰之木兰兮，

夕揽洲之宿莽。

O at dawn on slope magnolias I amass;
At eve at shoal I pick lodging-grass.

日月忽其不淹兮，

春与秋其代序。

O Sun and Moon, for e'er you turn and speed;
Spring and autumn each other succeed;

惟草木之零落兮，

恐美人之迟暮。

O there appear withering trees and grass;
I fear the beauty may fade, alas.

不抚壮而弃秽兮，

何不改乎此度？

O why not throw filth away while in prime?
Why not reform the system in time?

---

*magnolia: any of a genus (*Magnolia*) of trees or shrubs with barks like those of the cinnamon and with large, fragrant and usually showy flowers, a symbol of beauty and nobility.
*lodging-grass: a perennial aromatic grass extinct now, a coined term based on the motivation of Chinese sumang (su: lodging; mang: grass), said to be able to stand having its heart plucked away without dying, a symbol of fidelity, goodness and permanence.

乘骐骥以驰骋兮,

来吾道夫先路!

离骚

O please gallop astride your brawny steed;
Forward I'll go and the way I'll lead!

昔三后之纯粹兮,

固众芳之所在。

O the three kings were so pure and profound,
With all blossoms blossoming around.

---

*steed: a horse used or trained for riding: a spirited horse—sometimes used figuratively for something being likened to a horse. The use of horses in war can be traced back to the Shang dynasty (1600 B.C.-1046 B.C.), when a department of horse management was established. A verse from *the Book of Songs* tells of Lord Civil of Watch's industriousness: "In state affairs he leads; / He has three thousand steeds."

*the three kings: referring to Three Kings: the first kings of the three dynasties, Worm of Xia, Hotspring of Shang and King Civil of Zhou according to Yi Wang, an Eastern Han scholar.

杂申椒与菌桂兮,

岂惟纫夫蕙茝!

O those who love pepper and cassia there,
Can you match those who coumarous wear?

彼尧、舜之耿介兮,

既遵道而得路。

O Mound and Hibiscus, so fair and square,
They followed the Way, a thoroughfare.

---

*pepper: referring to Shen pepper or Sichuan pepper, popular as a spice. Because of its clustered red seeds, it has been used as a token of love and a symbol of fecundity since ancient times in China.
*cassia: any of a genus of herbs or shrubs, and trees of the caesalpinia family, common in tropical countries.
*coumarou: an aromatic herb, with leaves like hemp and square stems, red blooms and black seeds, smelling like selinea.
*Mound: Lord Mound (2,377 B.C.-2,259 B.C.), Yao if transliterated, a descendant of Lord Yellow (2717 B.C.-2599 B.C.). Divine and noble, Mound, who married his two daughters and demised his throne to Hibiscus, has been regarded as one of Five Lords in ancient China.
*Hibiscus: Shun if transliterated, an ancient sovereign, a descendant of Lord Yellow (2,717 B.C.-2,599 B.C.), a son-in-law of Mound (cir. 2,377 B.C.-2,259 B.C.), regarded as one of Five Lords in prehistoric China.
*the Way: the Kingly Way, the righteous tradition initiated by Lord Mound and Hibiscus in ancient Chinese government, directly inherited from the Way of Heaven, the natural or divine ultimate force in the cosmos, which is identifiable with the Word in *the Bible* or the Logos in Heraclitus's *Physis*.

8

绘画：沈子琪

何桀纣之昌披兮,

夫唯捷径以窘步。

O how evil, Stump and Chow their power swayed;
They sought a short cut but faltered and strayed.

惟夫党人之偷乐兮,

路幽昧以险隘。

O the gang indulge in pleasures on the sly;
Dim, dark is my way, where perils lie.

岂余身之殚殃兮,

恐皇舆之败绩。

O do I fear disasters fall to my pain?
I do fear the fall of our domain.

忽奔走以先后兮,

及前王之踵武。

O back and forth, I hurry and I run;
Lord, do catch up with our former one.

*Stump: Fowl Stump (?-1,600 B.C.), Jie if transliterated, the last king of the Xia dynasty, a tyrant, notorious for his debauchery and ebriosity.
*Chow: King Chow (cir. 1105 B.C.- 1046 B.C.) , also known as King Sen, the last king of the Shang dynasty, who reigned thirty years, a habitual drunkard and lecher, violent and atrocious as a tyrant who minced, parched or pickled his ministers.

10

荃不查余之中情兮，
反信谗而齌怒。

离骚

O my faithfulness you do not know much;
Hoodwinked by slander, you flame as such.

余固知謇謇之为患兮，
忍而不能舍也。

O I do know that remonstration can be a bane;
Howe'er, I could not myself refrain.

指九天以为正兮，
夫唯灵修之故也。

O Nine Heavens, do my rectitude test;
For my righteous lord I've done all my best.

曰黄昏以为期兮，
羌中道而改路。

O we pledged at dusk we would be combined,
But on the midway you changed your mind.

---

*Nine Heavens: the eight directions and center of the universe, or sometimes referred to as the the highest layer of the universe.

初既与余成言兮,

后悔遁而有他。

O there and then, you made the pledge to me,
But soon repented, and now you flee.

余既不难夫离别兮,

伤灵修之数化。

O I don't think our departure a great pain,
But you do change again and again.

余既滋兰之九畹兮,

又树蕙之百亩。

O eupatories I have grown in plots nine,
And scores of plots of tonka beans fine.

*tonka bean: an aromatic plant that contains coumarin, which is used as a flavoring in foods and tobacco, as well as a fragrance in cosmetics.

12

畦留夷与揭车兮，

杂杜衡与芳芷。

离骚

O I grow peony 'n auragrass abed;
Lo, asarums 'n angelicas spread.

冀枝叶之峻茂兮，

愿俟时乎吾将刈。

O I wish strong stems and leaves they could keep
Until the day when all of them I reap.

---

*peony: genus of about 30 species of perennial flowering plants (family *Paeoniaceae*) known for their large showy blossoms: pink, white, red or yellow. Outrageously beautiful in bloom with the fattest, most scrumptious flowers and lush green foliage, it is a symbol of elegance, nobility and prosperity in Chinese culture.
*auragrass: a coined term based on the attributes of the Chinese original jie che, said to be an aromatic herb, several feet tall, with white leaves and yellow flowers, growing at Pengton, once the capital of King Bosom (Huai) of Chu (?-206 B.C.) (a puppet king during Chu-Han Contention), now Copperhill (Tongshan) County and Xuzhou, Jiangsu Province.
*asarum: an evergreen aromatic herb growing on mountains, with heart-shaped leaves and small, dark purple flowers in winter, its tuber roots used as medicine.

虽萎绝其亦何伤兮,

哀众芳之芜秽。

O I grieve not if they fade and die away;
It hurts me if all of them decay.

众皆竞进以贪婪兮,

凭不厌乎求索。

O in lust and greediness they try their best;
For fame and richness, they strive and quest.

羌内恕己以量人兮,

各兴心而嫉妒。

O others they suspect, themselves they condone;
So jealous, they struggle for their own.

忽驰骛以追逐兮,

非余心之所急。

O they strive for all those they will acquire;
These, howe'er, are not what I desire.

老冉冉其将至兮,

恐修名之不立。

O step by step, old age is coming near,
But I'm not well established I fear.

朝饮木兰之坠露兮,

夕餐秋菊之落英。

离骚

O at dawn from magnolia leaves I drink dew;
At eve chrysanthemum petals I chew.

苟余情其信姱以练要兮,

长顑颔亦何伤。

O so long as I stay true and remain fair and square,
For my haggardness how can I care?

擥木根以结茝兮,

贯薜荔之落蕊。

O with a tree root angelicas I tie;
To lace climbing fig stamens I hie.

---

*chrysanthemum: any of a genus of perennials of the composite family, some cultivated varieties of which have large heads of showy flowers of various colors, a symbol of elegance and integrity in Chinese culture, one of the "four gents" sanctified in Chinese literature, which are wintersweet, orchid, bamboo, and chrysanthemum.
*climbing fig: pomelo fig, an evergreen vine with egg-shaped thick leaves two or three inches long, small flowers and fig-like fruit.

矫菌桂以纫蕙兮，

索胡绳之纚纚。

O with cassia sprays coumarous I twine,
And plait a garlic rope long and fine.

謇吾法夫前修兮，

非世俗之所服。

O I learn from the saints and sages of yore
What people today can do no more.

虽不周于今之人兮，

愿依彭咸之遗则。

O although incongruent with the world today,
I would follow Cord Peng's teaching and way.

长太息以掩涕兮，

哀民生之多艰。

O with a long sigh, I wipe away my tears;
How hard the folk's life is, months and years!

---

*garlic: a bulbous herb of the lily family, the strong smelling bulb of which is widely used as seasoning in meats, salads and so on.

*Cord Peng: Xian Peng if transliterated, a patriotic courtier in the Shang dynasty, who drowned himself after his failure in his remonstrance to his king. Yuan Qu (cir. 345 B.C.-286 B.C.), our patriotic poet, took him as an example and drowned himself as well.

余虽好修姱以鞿羁兮,

謇朝谇而夕替。

离骚

O although I'm self-disciplined, trying to be chaste,
At morn I counsel, at eve debased.

既替余以蕙纕兮,

又申之以揽茝。

O they curse me for the basil I wear
And then for my angelica fair.

亦余心之所善兮,

虽九死其犹未悔。

O to remain worthy and pure I try;
I won't regret e'en if nine times I'll die.

---

*basil: *Ocimum basilicum*, also called sweet basil, annual herb of the mint family (*Lamiaceae*), grown for its aromatic leaves. Basil is likely native to India and is widely grown as a kitchen herb. The leaves are used fresh or dried to flavour meats, fish, salads, and sauces; basil tea is a stimulant.

怨灵修之浩荡兮，

终不察夫民心。

O His Majesty's muddled, all complain;
He's so unconcerned with the folk's pain.

众女嫉余之蛾眉兮，

谣诼谓余以善淫。

O those ladies envy my eyebrows so good,
While accusing me of being so lewd.

固时俗之工巧兮，

偭规矩而改错。

O those flunkies hanker for a free ride;
They trespass the rules and ne'er abide.

背绳墨以追曲兮，

竞周容以为度。

O they conspire and scheme against the rule,
Craft or twisting as their common tool.

---

*His Majesty: referring to King Bosom (King Huai if transliterated) of Chu (-? 296 B.C.), the thirty-seventh monarch of Chu. He succeeded in defeating Way and exterminating Yue with the help of Yuan Qu but he gave up Yuan Qu's reforms half way, which finally caused the demise of his land.

忳郁邑余侘傺兮,

吾独穷困乎此时也。

离骚

O fretted, worried, gloomy, I feel distressed;
Why am I left alone, so trapped and so hard-pressed?

宁溘死以流亡兮,

余不忍为此态也。

O I would be exiled, I would rather die
Than surrender, wallowing in the sty.

鸷鸟之不群兮,

自前世而固然。

O the hawk will not flock with the wren;
It's the truth since the long past, since then.

---

*hawk: a diurnal bird of prey, notable for keen sight and strong flight, usually used as a metaphor for one who takes military means in contrast with a dove, one who tries to find peaceful solutions.
*wren: any of a variety of small, chunky, brownish birds (order *Passeriformes*), usually used as a metaphor for insignificant people or things.

何方圜之能周兮,

夫孰异道而相安?

O how can a circle fit in with a square?
How can they settle with no way to share?

屈心而抑志兮,

忍尤而攘诟。

O I check my heart, my will, my aim;
I bear all their reproach and blame!

伏清白以死直兮,

固前圣之所厚。

O I'd die for righteousness, so up raised,
As is what the ancient sages praised.

悔相道之不察兮,

延伫乎吾将反。

O the way I've failed to discern, alack;
After a while of doubt, I'll turn back.

回朕车以复路兮,

及行迷之未远。

O I veer my cart to the former way
Before I have gone further astray.

20

绘画：沈子琪

步余马于兰皋兮，

驰椒丘且焉止息。

O with my steed, the orchid bank I stroll
Till we come to rest at the Pepper Knoll.

进不入以离尤兮，

退将复修吾初服。

O having advanced, but accused of crime,
I'd retire to the past, the good old time.

制芰荷以为衣兮，

集芙蓉以为裳。

O I sew trapa and lotus as my gown;
With lotus flowers my garb I adorn.

---

*Pepper Knoll: name of a knoll and an ancient place bearing this name in today's Jiangxi Province.
*trapa: a floating water-plant with heart-shaped leaves and edible seeds of two, three or four prongs in autumn.
*lotus: one of the various plants of the waterlily family, noted for their large floating round leaves and showy flowers blooming in white or pink, a symbol of purity and elegance in Chinese culture, unsoiled though out of soil, so clean with all leaves green.

22

不吾知其亦已兮,

苟余情其信芳。

离骚

O if they don't understand me, they don't;
Fragrance inside, I won't sigh, I won't.

高余冠之岌岌兮,

长余佩之陆离。

O highly raised, raised high, I wear my crown;
Long, so long is the sash of my gown.

芳与泽其杂糅兮,

唯昭质其犹未亏。

O though fragrance and dirt together blend,
What we call integrity will not rend.

忽反顾以游目兮,

将往观乎四荒。

O I glance backward and afar I gaze;
To the four directions, the four ways!

佩缤纷其繁饰兮,

芳菲菲其弥章。

O so splendid clothes, in full array!
So fragrant blossoms, blossoms so gay!

民生各有所乐兮,

余独好修以为常。

O everyone has pleasures of his own;
I cultivate my virtue all alone.

虽体解吾犹未变兮,

岂余心之可惩。

O I won't change, e'en though my body may rend;
How can I falter or there suspend?

女媭之婵媛兮,

申申其詈予。

O my sister showing me concern
Exhorts me in a voice so stern:

24

曰：鲧婞直以亡身兮，
终然夭乎羽之野。

离骚

O Great Fish was straightforward and thereof died;
He was killed at Mt. Plume and thrown aside.

汝何博謇而好修兮，
纷独有此姱节。

O why are you so square, virtuous but obtuse?
Why stick to faithfulness? What's the use?

薋菉葹以盈室兮，
判独离而不服。

O caltrop and cocklebur fill the room;
Why do you keep off a common bloom?

---

*Great Fish: Kun if transliterated, father of Great Worm, the First King of Xia (21 B.C.-16 B.C.). Fish was executed by Hibiscus for his blundering failure to block the deluge during Lord Mound's reign.
*Mt. Plume: the earliest mountain mentioned in Chinese literature and history, in today's Jiangsu Province.
*caltrop: any of various plants (especially *Tribulus terrestris*) with spiny heads or fruit that entangle the feet.
*cocklebur: a low branching, rank weed (genus *Xanthium*) of the composite family, with hard ovoid or oblong two-celled burs about an inch long.

众不可户说兮,

孰云察余之中情?

O I can't talk to all at each door;
Who can understand my heart, my wherefore?

世并举而好朋兮,

夫何茕独而不予听?

O all the world will good companions be?
Why all alone, and why don't you listen to me?"

依前圣以节中兮,

喟凭心而历兹。

O I follow our saints to build my will;
Alas, indignant! I can't stay still!

济沅、湘以南征兮,

就重华而陈词:

O crossing the Yüan, old wisdom I'd seek;
Before Lord Hibiscus thus I speak:

启《九辩》与《九歌》兮,
夏康娱以自纵。

离骚

O Ope got *Nine Counts* and *Nine Songs*, and he
Indulged himself, going on the spree.

不顾难以图后兮,
五子用失乎家衖。

O no consequences could he foresee;
His prince Looker brought disorders to be.

**Nine Counts*: music which is believed to have been composed by Lord Hibiscus, before there came a long poem accredited to Jade Song, the author's student.
**Nine Songs*: music which is believed to have been composed by Lord Hibiscus, and later came a collection of psalms consisting of eleven cantos by the author himself.
*Looker: Martial Looker, Wuguan if transliterated, King Ope's fifth son, who caused a great dissension when trying to usurp the Xia throne.

羿淫游以佚畋兮,

又好射夫封狐。

O Archer to hunting gave his free will,
And great foxes he would love to kill.

固乱流其鲜终兮,

浞又贪夫厥家。

O no good end for those having a loose life,
Soak Cold killed Archer and took his wife.

浇身被服强圉兮,

纵欲而不忍。

O Pour Cold relied on his violent strain;
His great lust he did not constrain.

日康娱而自忘兮,

厥首用夫颠陨。

O he made merry all day and forgot all
And at last caused his own head to fall.

---

*Archer: King Archer, Houyi if transliterated, a legendary figure in Chinese myths. In Mound's age, there were ten suns in the sky, making everything hard to survive. To save the people, King Archer shot off nine of them
*Soak Cold: Soak (cir. 2013 B. C.-1933 B.C.), surnamed Cold, a usurper of the Xia throne.
*Pour Cold: Soak Cold's son, a man of great physical strength, said to be able to propel a boat on land.

28

夏桀之常违兮,

乃遂焉而逢殃。

离骚

O Stump went against the usual way,
So to banes and pains he could but stray.

后辛之菹醢兮,

殷宗用而不长。

O King Sen made his foe into meat paste;
So his dynasty fell, to lie waste.

---

*King Sen: also known as King Chow (cir. 1105 B.C.-1046 B.C.), the last king of the Shang dynasty, regarded as a tyrant, who pickled, minced and parched his vassals and courtiers.

汤、禹俨而祗敬兮,

周论道而莫差。

O Hotspring and Worm were just, full of respect;
King Civil kept the Way, circumspect.

举贤才而授能兮,

循绳墨而不颇。

O raised were the wise, and employed the adept;
Nothing went amiss, the rule well kept.

皇天无私阿兮,

览民德焉错辅。

O Heaven was fair to all, every sort;
All virtuous men could have His support.

---

*Hotspring: Tang if transliterated, King of Shang (cir. 1,670 B.C.-1,587 B.C.), the founding king of Shang, who annihilated Xia with the help of two talents Captain and Zhonghui as his two prime ministers.
*Worm: Yu if transliterated, formally addressed Lord Worm, the founding father of Xia, who took over the leadership from Hibiscus. It was said that Mound was put in jail, having lost his morality, and Hibiscus died in a moor when he was in a tour. The poet borrowed the ancient legend to imply that King Bosom of Chu's reign was in danger of being destroyed.
*King Civil: King Civil of Zhou (1,152 B.C.-1,056 B.C.), a wise monarch of high reputation in Chinese history, reigning as Lord of West, a vassal state under Shang, and saliently remembered as the designer of Octagram and the founder of Zhou (1046 B.C.-256 B.C.).

夫维圣哲以茂行兮,

苟得用此下土。

O only when saintly lords had greater worth
Could they have the right for the good earth.

瞻前而顾后兮,

相观民之计极。

O look forward and have a backward view,
You can know what all people should do.

夫孰非义而可用兮?

孰非善而可服?

O what kind of injustice can one take part in?
How can one fall down to commit sin?

阽余身而危死兮,

览余初其犹未悔。

O though the risk of life threatens a kill,
I ne'er regret and will ne'er change my will.

绘画：沈子琪

不量凿而正枘兮,

固前修以菹醢。

O mortise not gauged, a tenon they make;
The lords minced and parched, what a mistake.

曾歔欷余郁邑兮,

哀朕时之不当。

O I sigh to my grief and to my sore;
The misfortunate time I deplore.

揽茹蕙以掩涕兮,

沾余襟之浪浪。

O with a basil leaf I sweep tears down,
And the tears drop off to wet my gown.

---

*basil leaf: glossy and oval-shaped, with smooth or slightly toothed edges that typically cup slightly; the leaves are arranged oppositely along the square stems.

跪敷衽以陈辞兮，

耿吾既得此中正。

O lapel oped, I speak, fallen on knees;
The righteousness in heart does me ease.

驷玉虬以桀鹥兮，

溘埃风余上征。

O I drive Phoenix Cart pulled by Jade Steed
And in dust to the Heavens we speed.

朝发轫于苍梧兮，

夕余至乎县圃。

O at dawn I leave the south at Mt. Green
And at dusk I arrive at Mt. Queen.

---

*Phoenix Cart: a fabulous cart taken by a fairy or immortal in Chinese mythology or a cart for a sovereign, driven by four fine horses with four bits and eight bells.
*Jade Steed: a fine horse so named.
*Mt. Green: also known as Mt. Nine Doubts, where is Lord Hibiscus's tomb.
*Mt. Queen: Mt. Kunlun if transliterated, the most sacred mountain in China. It starts from the eastern Pamir Plateau, stretches across New Land (Xinjiang) and Tibet, and extends to Blue Sea (Qinghai), with an average altitude of 5,500-6000 meters. In Chinese myths, Mt. Queen is where lives Queen Mother or called Mother West, a sovereign goddess.

34

欲少留此灵琐兮,

日忽忽其将暮。

离骚

O at Gate Tower there I'd take a short rest,
But the sun is setting in the west.

吾令羲和弭节兮,

望崦嵫而勿迫。

O I bid She-her forward: Slowly run,
Don't rush to Mt. Steep to greet the sun.

路漫漫其修远兮,

吾将上下而求索。

O the roadway rolls on to twist and turn;
I'll seek and search, up and down I yearn.

---

*She-her: Xihe if transliterated, the mother of the sun or the dyad of Goddess of Sun and Goddess of Calendar in Chinese mythology, and the driver of Sun's car drawn by six dragons according to another source.
*Mt. Steep: a mountain or a range of mountains into which the suns are said to set in Chinese mythology.

饮余马于咸池兮，

总余辔乎扶桑。

O at Cord Pool there I let my horse free
And tie it to Fuguesome, the giant tree.

折若木以拂日兮，

聊逍遥以相羊。

O with a Fugueome twig the sun I brush
So I can stroll on, as there's no rush.

前望舒使先驱兮，

后飞廉使奔属。

O in front I let Wansue slowly run
So that Flydeer can catch up anon.

---

*Cord Pool: a pool where the suns take their baths in Chinese mythology.
*Fuguesome: Fusang if transliterated, a great fairy tree, which the sun rises against according to Chinese mythology, also known as Lithe Tree. It has leaves and berries like a mulberry tree, but it is much bigger, as can be six thousand meters tall and six thousand armfuls in girth.
*Wansue: Wangsu if transliterated, an immortal who drives a cart for Luna, Goddess of the Moon, in Chinese mythology.
*Flydeer: Feilian if transliterated, God of Wind in Chinese mythology, which is said to be a flying deer with a bird's head.

鸾皇为余先戒兮，

雷师告余以未具。

O Queen Phoenix keeps vigilance ahead;
Not yet ready, Lord Thunder says instead.

吾令凤鸟飞腾兮，

继之以日夜。

O I order the phoenix to take flight
Night after day, day after night.

飘风屯其相离兮，

帅云霓而来御。

O fluttering with winds, she whirls to flee
While the hued clouds brought in beam to me.

---

*Queen Phoenix: referring to a certain phoenix. In Chinese mythology, the most beautiful bird, the phoenix, only perches on phoenix trees, i.e. firmiana, only eats firmiana fruit, and only drinks sweet spring water, and this mythic bird appears only in times of peace and sagacious rule and lives for ever through cycles of nirvana.

*Lord Thunder: a deity with a human head and a dragon's body, whose stomach produces thunder when agitated.

纷总总其离合兮,

斑陆离其上下。

O the clouds float, disappear and appear,
Dispersing up and down, there and here.

吾令帝阍开关兮,

倚阊阖而望予。

O I ask a guard to open the door,
Against the tower he stares and stares more.

时暧暧其将罢兮,

结幽兰而延伫。

O it's getting dark as now ends the day;
With wrung orchids I linger to stay.

世溷浊而不分兮,

好蔽美而嫉妒。

O so limpid or turbid, they can't tell,
Despising all those who can do well.

38

朝吾将济于白水兮，

登阆风而绁马。

离骚

O at dawn I'll get across the River White,
And climb High Wind to tie my horse tight.

忽反顾以流涕兮，

哀高丘之无女。

O I sudd'nly look back and my tears flow;
No belle on the High Knoll, there is no.

溘吾游此春宫兮，

折琼枝以继佩。

O I have come to Spring Palace to play
And adorn myself with a jade spray.

---

*the River White: name of a river in Chinese mythology, originating from Mt. Queen. One will become immortal after drinking water from it.
*High Wind: an abode for immortals on top of Mt. Queen, which has three strata of precipices, and from which the River White flows.
*the High Knoll: name of a mountain in the State of Chu.
*Spring Palace: the palace for Blue God in the East.

及荣华之未落兮，

相下女之可诒。

O before blossoms on the jade spray fade,
I'd find one to whom it can be paid.

吾令丰隆乘云兮，

求宓妃之所在。

O I bid Rich Plump start the cart to ride
To find where Miss Sedate does abide.

解佩纕以结言兮，

吾令謇修以为理。

O with my sash my proposal's wrapped in,
I ask Lame Right to be my go-between.

纷总总其离合兮，

忽纬繣其难迁。

O hazing clouds gather and they float on;
Soon I know the thing cannot be done.

---

*Rich Plump: God of Clouds, often referring to thunder in Chinese culture.
*Miss Sedate: Hidden Spirit's daughter, a goddess. According to legend, she got drowned in the Luo River, so enamored with the scenery on the banks, and was therefore made the spirit of the river, hence also known as Goddess of the Luo River.
*Lame Right: a go-between, said to be a courtier of Hidden Spirit (Fuxi, also known as Great Sky).

40

夕归次于穷石兮,

朝濯发乎洧盘。

离骚

O at dusk Sedate goes to Bow Stone there;
At dawn Wetpan sees her wash her hair.

保厥美以骄傲兮,

日康娱以淫游。

O counting on her charm she's full of pride;
To her there is no pleasure denied.

虽信美而无礼兮,

来违弃而改求。

O she, though charming, does not keep the rite;
Give her up, I'll look for my Miss Right.

---

*Bow Stone: a mountain in East China, where King Archer, bowmen's descendant, lived. Bow is also the short name of the State of Bowmen, a vassal state under Xia, in today's Shandong Peninsula.
*Wetpan: Weipan if transliterated, name of a river issuing from Mt. Steep in Chinese mythology.
*Miss Right: an uncertain ideal model of a bride or wife in contrast with Mr. Right.

览相观于四极兮，

周流乎天余乃下。

O I glance and gaze round at every end,
And after my tour there I now descend.

望瑶台之偃蹇兮，

见有娀之佚女。

O peering down at the top of Mt. Jade,
I see there the beautiful Song maid.

吾令鸩为媒兮，

鸩告余以不好。

I ask Poison: "Please my go-between be."
She's not that good, Poison so tells me.

*Mt. Jade: a mountain made of, or teeming with, jade.
*the beautiful Song maid: referring to Jane Plume, a beautiful princess from the State of Song, Lord Call's second concubine and Deeds' mother.
*Poison: name of a pernicious bird with plumes of deadly poison, a wrong go-between.

42

雄鸠之鸣逝兮，

余犹恶其佻巧。

离骚

O a turtle cries and will there soar;
Its artfulness and craft I abhor.

心犹豫而狐疑兮，

欲自适而不可。

O I hesitate, I pace to and fro;
I would go myself, oh, should I go?

凤皇既受诒兮，

恐高辛之先我。

O with bride-price Phoenix I entrust;
High Sen may have gone earlier, he must.

---

*turtle: turtledove, any of several small, wild, African and Eurasian pigeons (genus *Streptopelia* and especially *S. turtur*) noted for plaintive cooing and well known for its affection for mate and young.
*High Sen: referring to Lord Call, Lord Yellow's great-grandson, born at High Sen, that is, today's High Sen (Gaoxin), Shang Knoll (Shangqiu), Henan Province. He succeeded Lord High Sun and reigned 70 years, from 2436 B.C. to 2366 B.C..

欲远集而无所止兮，

聊浮游以逍遥。

O I'd go afar but settled I can't be,
So I just wander and loiter free.

及少康之未家兮，

留有虞之二姚。

O Young Prime's not yet married, not yet due;
There still remain two beauties from Yu.

理弱而媒拙兮，

恐导言之不固。

O the match-maker is not smart, nope!
For the success there is no much hope.

世溷浊而嫉贤兮，

好蔽美而称恶。

O the world chaotic, sages are despised;
Evils are praised and chasteness chastised.

---

*Young Prime: Shaokang if transliterated, the sixth king of the Xia dynasty, the inventor of Chinese wine.
*Yu: the State of Yu founded by Lord Hibiscus, which evolved into a major city in the Xia dynasty (cir. 21Century B.C.-16 Century B.C.), that is, today's Yu County, Henan Province. In the early Xia dynasty, the place was enfeoffed by Worm to Hibiscus's son, which was known as the State of Yu again. When Hotspring (cir. 1,670 B.C.-1,587 B.C.) founded Shang after having exterminated Xia , he made this place his capital.

闺中既以邃远兮,

哲王又不寤。

离骚

O to approach the belle is a hard thing;
Asleep is the sagacious king!

怀朕情而不发兮,

余焉能忍而与此终古?

O my love I can't express, can't declare.
How can I put up with this and live with this for e'er?

索琼茅以筳篿兮,

命灵氛为余占之。

O I find bindweeds and bamboo splints fine
And ask the wizard for me to divine.

曰:"两美其必合兮,

孰信修而慕之?

He says," O two beauties may come and combine;
Why don't they, just and virtuous, entwine?

---

*bindweed: any of several vines of the genera *Convolvulus* and *Calystegia* having a twining habit.

思九州之博大兮,

岂惟是其有女?"

O the land is so broad and vast you see;
Good ladies anywhere there can be!"

曰:"勉远逝而无狐疑兮,

孰求美而释女?

He says, "O do go ahead, go ahead without doubt.
Who will chase you up and kick you out?

何所独无芳草兮,

尔何怀乎故宇?"

O where can't you the fragrance of grass find?
Why are you just to your land confined?"

世幽昧以眩曜兮,

孰云察余之善恶?

O this world's so dark and does demons brood;
Who can distinguish evils from the good?

民好恶其不同兮,

惟此党人其独异!

O good or bad, men are of a different kind;
But this clique to falsehood is more inclined!

户服艾以盈要兮,

谓幽兰其不可佩。

O everyone wears warmwood on the waist;
Who says green orchids are not flowers chaste?

览察草木其犹未得兮,

岂珵美之能当?

O if you cannot tell good grass from bad grass,
How can you distinguish bronze from brass?

苏粪壤以充帏兮,

谓申椒其不芳。

O you fill your perfume sachet with dung,
But say your pepper smells bad. It's wrong.

欲从灵氛之吉占兮,

心犹豫而狐疑。

O I would hear the divination: correct,
But I hesitate and I suspect.

---

*warmwood: *Artemisia absinthium*, a perennial herb that has been historically used in absinthe and long thought to cause hallucinations.

绘画：沈子琪

48

巫咸将夕降兮,

怀椒糈而要之。

离骚

O the wizard will descend tonight;
To peppery rice I'll him invite.

百神翳其备降兮,

九疑缤其并迎。

O all the gods desend, shading the sun;
To meet them, from Nine Doubts the ghosts run.

皇剡剡其扬灵兮,

告余以吉故。

O their wisdom shines to show what's divine;
The wizard tells me good news, fine.

---

*peppery rice: rice spiced with pepper, like today's zongzi, pyramid-shaped dumpling made of glutinous rice wrapped in bamboo or reed leaves. Pepper, *Zanthoxylum bungeanum*, is a kind of spice called Chinese prickly ash, and rice, a type of cereal and food, eaten as staple food in many parts of Asia.
*Nine Doubts: Mt. Nine Doubts, the mountain where Hibiscus's body was buried. It was so named because it confused people by similar peaks and landscape.

曰:"勉升降以上下兮,

求矩矱之所同。

He says, "O you should go up and down to pursue
One who can share weal and woe with you.

汤、禹俨而求合兮,

挚、咎繇而能调。

O with Hotspring and Worm you can combine;
Hold and Moor can coordinate fine.

苟中情其好修兮,

又何必用夫行媒?

O if you are chaste and if you are clean,
Why must you look for a go-between?

---

*Hold: alias of Captain (Yin Yi) (1,649 B.C.-1,550 B.C.), a statesman, thinker, founding commander of Shang, and one of the founders of Wordism.
*Moor: Moor Potter (cir. 2,219 B.C.-2,113 B.C.), Gaoyao if transliterated, a great statesman, thinker, and educator throughout the era of Mound, Hibiscus and Worm, recognized by historians as Father of Justice, i.e. the originator of Chinese judicature, and regarded as one of the Four Sages of ancient times, along with the three great kings: Mound, Hibiscus and Worm.

50

说操筑于傅岩兮,

武丁用而不疑。

O Joy was once a mason at Fu's Stone;
King Wuding used him as a friend boon.

吕望之鼓刀兮,

遭周文而得举。

O Great Grand, a butcher in those days,
King Civil of Zhou did him up raise.

---

*Joy: Master Joy, Joy Fu, Yue Fu if transliterated, a noble minister of high reputation in the early Shang dynasty. Historic records say that the King of Shang dreamed of a sage, and he sent people out to search for him and found Joy, who was working at laying mud walls as a convict in servitude at Fu's Stone.
*Fu's Stone: also called Fu's Crag, so named because Joy Fu, a minister in the Shang dynasty, once worked here as a convict, east of today's Level Land (Pinglu) County, Shanxi Province.
*King Wuding: King Wuding (1250 B.C.-1,192 B.C.), the twenty-third king of Shang, one of the most capable sovereigns in its history. Under his governance, Shang prospered in all aspects.
*Great Grand: referring to Ziya Jiang, an influential strategist and statesman. Though he was a butcher at his young age, Great Grand remained diligent in hardship, expecting to display his ability for the country one day, but he did not make any achievement before he was 70 years old. He went west at the age of 72, fishing as he waited for King Civil, and finally won his appreciation.
*King Civil: King Civil (1,152 B.C.-1,056 B.C.), a wise monarch of high reputation, remembered as the founder of Zhou, the third imperial suzerain in Chinese history.

宁戚之讴歌兮,

齐桓闻以该辅。

O Peace chanted with his ox-horn, great;
Lord of Qi asked him to help the state.

及年岁之未晏兮,

时亦犹其未央。

O go and achieve while you are in prime;
Use your talent and cherish your time.

恐鹈鴂之先鸣兮,

使夫百草为之不芳。"

O I fear, too early the cuckoos cry;
All grasses are thereby rendered to fade, so dry."

---

*Peace: a meritorious statesman of Qi in the Spring and Autumn period. In his early age, Peace was poor and had no access to officialdom. When Lord Column of Qi passed by, Peace knocked on an ox horn and sang out his frustration and attracted the lord's attention.

*Lord of Qi: Lord Column of Qi (?-643 B.C.), the sixteenth monarch of the State of Qi, the leader of the Five Hegemons in the Autumn and Spring Period.

*cuckoo: any of a family of birds with a long, slender body, grayish-brown on top and white below, a symbol of sadness in Chinese culture. It is said that during the Shang dynasty, Cuckoo (Yu Du), a caring king of the State of Shu, abdicated the throne due to a flood and lived in reclusion. After his death, he, the human Cuckoo, turned into a bird cuckoo, wailing day and night, shedding tears and blood.

何琼佩之偃蹇兮,

众薆然而蔽之。

O what clinking pendant, what precious jade!
Why will all people its lustre shade?

惟此党人之不谅兮,

恐嫉妒而折之。

O how wicked this gang of people can be!
Out of jealousy they may break me!

时缤纷其变易兮,

又何可以淹留?

O wayward the crowd and fickle the throng!
How can I linger here for so long?

兰芷变而不芳兮，

荃蕙化而为茅。

O orchids 'n angelica lose their charm;
Calamus 'n tonka beans sprawl to harm.

何昔日之芳草兮，

今直为此萧艾也？

O why has yesterday's fragrance of grass
Turned into warmwood 'n mugwort? Alas!

岂其有他故兮，

莫好修之害也！

O have we other reasons to find?
They've not been made into the good kind!

---

*tonka bean: a tropical tree native to South America, *Dipteryx odorata*, having pulpy, egg-shaped, one-seeded pods and fragrant seeds used as medicine and as a substitute for vanilla and for flavoring tobacco and candies.
*mugwort: a temperate perennial herbaceous plant, *Artemisia vulgaris*, with aromatic leaves and clusters of small greenish-white flowers, used in traditional systems of medicine.

余以兰为可恃兮，
羌无实而容长。

离骚

O thoroughwort's trusty I used to think;
It bears no fruit and can smell so stink!

委厥美以从俗兮，
苟得列乎众芳。

O it follows the vain world without grace
And mid flowers its fragrance does debase.

椒专佞以慢慆兮，
樧又欲充夫佩帏。

O the pepper flatters, looking of pride;
The cornel will fill the sachet to bide.

---

*thoroughwort: a stout, fragrant hairy herb, the boneset, 2 to 5 feet high, having opposite mostly oblong leaves and an open cymose cluster of white flower heads.
*cornel: a kind of dogwood carried or worn to exorcize evil spirits especially on Double Ninth Day, as is traditionally believed.

既干进而务入兮，

又何芳之能祇？

O they speculate a lot, to be sure;
How can they stay innocent and pure?

固时俗之流从兮，

又孰能无变化？

O the vulgar world changes, always fluid;
Whoe'er can retain his rectitude?

览椒兰其若兹兮，

又况揭车与江离？

O pepper and thoroughwort changed so much,
Will plantains and selinea stay as such?

惟兹佩之可贵兮，

委厥美而历兹。

O only my trinkets so precious stay;
Their value remains until today.

芳菲菲而难亏兮，

芬至今犹未沫。

O their fragrance is hard to dissipate;
E'en now the scent does not alleviate.

和调度以自娱兮,

聊浮游而求女。

离骚

O with temperance in pleasure I dwell,
Thereby I stroll to look for a belle.

及余饰之方壮兮,

周流观乎上下。

O my pendants still boast of their great worth,
Wherewith I will tour Heaven and earth.

灵氛既告余以吉占兮,

历吉日乎吾将行。

O the wizard's told me about the auspicious day;
I'll get prepared and start right away.

折琼枝以为羞兮,

精琼爢以为粮。

O I break off green twigs for meat air-dried,
And grind jadeite as food to provide.

为余驾飞龙兮，

杂瑶象以为车。

O give me a dragon, and I'll depart;
All jewels and ivory fill my cart.

何离心之可同兮？

吾将远逝以自疏。

O If one's discordant, how can we team;
I will go far away and estrange him.

邅吾道夫昆仑兮，

路修远以周流。

O to Mt. Queen I will swerve for a tour;
It's far away so I'll check for sure.

扬云霓之晻蔼兮，

鸣玉鸾之啾啾。

O to hued clouds and mist the sun does sink;
The car bell sways to and fro to clink.

朝发轫于天津兮，

夕余至乎西极。

O at dawn from Heaven's Ford there I start;
At eve I will reach the westmost part.

---

*Heaven's Ford: a ford on the Silver River in Chinese mythology, i.e. the Milky Way.

凤皇翼其承旗兮,

高翱翔之翼翼。

离骚

O the hued phoenix o'er the flags does fly,
Its plumage fluttering in the sky.

忽吾行此流沙兮,

遵赤水而容与。

O I rush to the quick sand prone to flow
And go along the Red, going slow.

---

*phoenix: a legendary bird which is supposed to live 500 years, burn itself to ashes on a pyre, and rise alive from the ashes to live another period. Phoenixes are auspicious birds; unlike ordinary ones, they only perch on parasol trees, and only eat bamboo shoots and pearly stone. The phoenix, like the dragon, is a totem of the Chinese nation, accepted as the symbol of Chu in particular.
*the Red: the Red River, a river in Chinese mythology, which originates from Mt. Queen, running from the southeast of the mountain eastward into the Yellow River.

麾蛟龙使梁津兮,

诏西皇使涉予。

O I ask Dragon to build a bridge now;
"Lord West, ferry me, no matter how."

路修远以多艰兮,

腾众车使径待。

O the road rolls long, and it is so hard;
All the carts wait by the road on guard.

路不周以左转兮,

指西海以为期。

O I turn left when passing Mt. Non-Round,
For West Sea, the destination, bound.

---

*Dragon: name of a certain dragon. The dragon, a serpent-like giant winged animal that can change its girth and length, has been worshiped as a totem of the Chinese nation, a symbol of benevolence and sovereignty in Chinese culture.
*Lord West: Young Sky, Shaohao if transliterated, God of West Sky living in the west in Chinese mythology, Lord Yellow's son in history, one of the Five Sovereigns.
*Mt. Non-Round: also called Mt. Broken, a mountain in Chinese mythology. According to *Seas and Mountains*, the earliest geography book in China, Co-work (Gonggong) butted the mountain with his head in anger, so it was was broken, hence the name.
*West Sea: a sea in the west in Chinese mythology.

屯余车其千乘兮,

齐玉轪而并驰。

离骚

O a thousand carts I gather, ideal;
We will gallop forward wheel to wheel.

驾八龙之婉婉兮,

载云旗之委蛇。

O the eight steeds graciously run ahead;
The clouded banners unfurl to spread.

抑志而弭节兮,

神高驰之邈邈。

O composed, silent, I go step by step
While my thought flies so high, full of pep.

奏《九歌》而舞《韶》兮,

聊假日以偷乐。

O *Nine Songs* I now play, *Fair* I now dance;
Come on, these are good hours for romance.

---

*Nine Songs: a collection of Yuan Qu's eleven psalms.
*Fair: a famous piece of music composed by Lord Hibiscus, dance cantata, played with Pandean pipes.

陟升皇之赫戏兮,

忽临睨夫旧乡。

O the sun rises east, a pool of gleam;
I see my hometown just like a dream.

仆夫悲余马怀兮,

蜷局顾而不行。

O my groom feels sad, my horse hurts, alack;
They cower and cringe, and now they turn back.

乱曰：已矣哉！

The finale says, It's all over now!

国无人莫我知兮,

又何怀乎故都！

O if no fellow does me understand,
Why am I so concerned with my land?

既莫足与为美政兮,

吾将从彭咸之所居！

O if I can't fulfill my Beauteous Deal's goal,
I'll go to Cord Peng's abode to appease my soul.

---

*Beauteous Deal: a governmental program proposed and designed by Yuan Qu to select officials based on good virtue and ability so as to rejuvenate the State of Chu.

九歌

Nine Songs

东皇太一
Great One, Our East Lord

九歌

吉日兮辰良,

穆将愉兮上皇;

A blessed hour, o a good day,
To August Lord o respects I pay.

抚长剑兮玉珥,

璆锵鸣兮琳琅。

I stroke my long sword, o sheath ears blink;
My pendants cling-clang, o trinkets clink.

---

*Great One: name of a star, the Supreme God of Heaven, the noblest God of Heaven, also known as East Lord because its shrine is located in the east of the State of Chu. Besides, it is an abstract philosophical concept in the first place, referring to the Word or the One that creates everything.
*August Lord: referring to Great One, Lord East.
*sheath ear: what is usually called tsuba, which is a transliteration from Japanese, the protruding part of a sheath, also called sword ear or sword nose.

瑶席兮玉瑱,

盍将把兮琼芳;

The jewel mat, o the jade weight;
The flowers in our hand o smell so great.

蕙肴蒸兮兰藉,

奠桂酒兮椒浆。

Beneath basil, o tonka bean meat;
Pepper brew fine, o laurel wine sweet.

---

*jade weight: a pressure gem, a rare gem baton held by the king or laid before him on the table, signifying the weight and steadiness of his rule, one foot and two inches long, with the symbolizing mountains of the four compasses carved on it.
*tonka bean meat: meat spiced with aromatic seeds from a tropical tree known as the coumarou.
*basil: any of several aromatic herbs belonging to the genus *Ocimum*, of the mint family: prized for its savory green leaves. Sweet basil (*O. basilicum*) has more than 150 culinary cultivars, including the tiny-leafed bush basil, the large-leafed mammoth basil, and the purple-leafed dark opal basil.
*pepper: referring to pepper from the ancient State of Shen, also known as Qin pepper or Chinese pepper, widely used as a spice. Because of clustered red seeds, it has been a symbol of fecundity since ancient times in China.
*pepper brew: a good quality liquor seasoned with a kind of Sichuan pepper.
*laurel: *laurus nobilis*, an evergreen shrub with aromatic, lance-shaped leaves, yellowish flowers, and succulent, cherry-like fruit, a symbol of glory usually in the form of a crown or wreath of laurel to indicate honor or high merit.
*laurel wine: wine seasoned with the essences of laurel flowers.

九歌

扬枹兮拊鼓,

Drumstick raised, o drum, strong, strong!

疏缓节兮安歌,
陈竽瑟兮浩倡。

The beats are gentle, o a slow song;
The flute and zither tunes o linger long.

灵偃蹇兮姣服,
芳菲菲兮满堂;

The wizard dances o in costume;
The great hall is filled o with perfume.

五音纷兮繁会,
君欣欣兮乐康。

Five notes of music o in accord,
So happy, merry, o bless my lord.

---

*five notes: referring to the pentatonic scale of Chinese music, i.e. Gong, Shang, Jiao, Zhi and Yu, equivalent to Do, Re, Mi, Sol, La in western music.

绘画：沈子琪

云中君

Lord in Clouds

九歌

浴兰汤兮沐芳,

华采衣兮若英。

I bathe in scented spring o in steam;
And put on a bright coat o to gleam.

灵连蜷兮既留,

烂昭昭兮未央。

The wizard possessed o does descend,
Flashing and flashing o without end.

蹇将憺兮寿宫,

与日月兮齐光。

For the rite you'll come o to the shrine,
The sun and the moon o vie to shine.

---

*Lords in Clouds: referring to Luna or God of Clouds, also known as Rich Plump, for example in *Woebegone*.

*scented spring: hotspring where one may take a bath, which may be scented with a kind of aromatic herb like eupatories.

龙驾兮帝服，

聊翱游兮周章。

Well-dressed, you ride o the cart
To soar high and watch o every part.

灵皇皇兮既降，

猋远举兮云中。

A graceful soul lights o there to ray,
And then in the clouds o hides away.

览冀州兮有余，

横四海兮焉穷。

Your brilliance twinkles o o'er the land
While you tour around o to command.

思夫君兮太息，

极劳心兮忡忡。

I miss you and heave o a long sigh;
So obsessed with you, o what a try!

---

the land: referring to Middle Kingdom or Middle Land, also called Grand-Great (Huaxia), the traditional proper name of China, which conveys to its posterity the greatness of its culture and glory as well as rites and justice. The word China might be a transliteration of Qin Jin, either a vassal state under Zhou's suzerainty.

湘君

Lord of Xiang

君不行兮夷犹,

蹇谁留兮中洲;

You do not come here o but there stroll;
For whom rest you there o on the shoal?

美要眇兮宜修,

沛吾乘兮桂舟;

I dress myself up o though I glow;
The waves lick my boat o while I row.

令沅湘兮无波,

使江水兮安流;

The Yuan and Xiang flow, o of waves free;
Run gently, gently, o peaceful be.

望夫君兮未来,

吹参差兮谁思;

I gaze far away, o there you stay;
Whom do I crave for? O my flute play!

---

*Lord of Xiang: God of the River Xiang, often referred to as the spirit of Hibiscus.
*the Yuan and Xiang: the Yuan River and the Xiang River both flowing to Lake Cavehall, the two big rivers mainly in today's Hunan Province.

九歌

驾飞龙兮北征,

邅吾道兮洞庭;

I drive my boat north o so fast now;
I'll reach Lake Cavehall, o veered my prow.

薜荔柏兮蕙绸,

荪桡兮兰旌;

Screen of climbing fig, o tent of straw;
Orchid flag, o cassia oar!

---

*Lake Cavehall: a large lake with an area of 2,740 square kilometers, a lake of strategic importance since ancient times, a place of many resources and cultural legacies in today's Hunan Province.
*climbing fig: alias pomelo fig, an aromatic vine bearing fig-like fruit.
*orchid: any of a widely distributed family of terrestrial or epiphytic monocotyledonous plants having thickened bulbous roots and often very showy distinctive flowers.
*cassia: any of a genus of herbs or shrubs, and trees of the caesalpinia family, common in tropical countries.

望涔阳兮极浦，

横大江兮扬灵；

Rainshine Route ashore, o there I gaze;
To cross the current, o sails they raise.

扬灵兮未极，

女婵媛兮为余太息；

Fleet, I don't see o your trace;
Who sighs o'er there for me? O the girl of grace.

横流涕兮潺湲，

隐思君兮陫侧；

I can't stop my tears; o they will flow;
Painfully, I croon o just for you.

桂棹兮兰枻，

斲冰兮积雪；

Helm and oar, o fast I ply;
From cut ice o snow does fly.

---

*Rainshine Route: an important post road south of the Long River, in the area of today's Li County, Hunan Province.

采薜荔兮水中，
搴芙蓉兮木末；

九歌

Climbing fig's gathered o in a sea？！
Lotus flowers are picked o from a tree？！

心不同兮媒劳，
恩不甚兮轻绝；

We don't share a heart, o no concern;
I would show my love, o this you spurn

石濑兮浅浅，
飞龙兮翩翩；

The stone stream's swift, o but right;
The boat flies on, o so light.

---

*lotus: one of the various plants of the waterlily family, provincial for their large floating round leaves and showy flowers, especially the white or pink Asian lotus, used as a religious symbol in Hinduism and Buddhism. And in Chinese culture, it is a symbol of purity and elegance, unsoiled though out of soil, so clean with all leaves green.

交不忠兮怨长,

期不信兮告余以不闲;

Not faithful in love, o you hate me;
You don't keep your promise, o you say you are not free.

朝骋骛兮江皋,

夕弭节兮北渚;

At dawn I run fast o on the shore;
At eve I stop north, o there I moor.

鸟次兮屋上,

水周兮堂下;

On the roof, o the birds cheep;
Neath the hall, o the waves leap.

捐余玦兮江中,

遗余佩兮醴浦;

I throw my jade ring o to the pour,
And lay my pendant o on the shore.

---

*jade ring: a jewel worn by nobles in ancient China.

九歌

采芳洲兮杜若,

将以遗兮下女;

At the shoal I pick o pollia grass;
And this I'll present o to the lass.

时不可兮再得,

聊逍遥兮容与。

Time flies like a dart, o no return;
Do rest reassured o while you yearn.

---

*pollia: a perennial herb with horizontal long rhizomes and erect or ascending stems, 30-50 cm tall and 3-8 mm thick, puberulent, and blowing actinomorphic flowers.

湘夫人

Lady of Xiang

帝子降兮北渚,
目眇眇兮愁予;

This lady does light o on North Shoal;
She attracts my eyes, o lures my soul.

袅袅兮秋风,
洞庭波兮木叶下;

Autumn wind, o sough and sough;
Lake Cavehall sees tree leaves o falling now.

登白薠兮骋望,
与佳期兮夕张;

Having climbed Scirpus, o far I gaze;
Shall we meet at eve o in this place?

---

*Lady of Xiang: Mound's younger daughter and Hibiscus's queen or imperial concubine, who became Goddess of the Xiang River after being drowned therein.
*North Shoal: a shoal in the north of Lake Cavehall, the second largest freshwater lake in China.
*Lake Cavehall: a lake in present-day Hunan Province, with an area of 3,879.2 square kilometers and 803.2 kilometers in circumference, rich with natural resources and cultural attractions.
*Scirpus: probably a mound or hill covered with scirpus, which is *Scirpus triangulatus*, a large genus of widely distributed annual or perennial sedge (family *Cyperaceae*) that bear solitary or much-clustered spikelets containing perfect flowers with a perianth of bristles.

九歌

鸟何萃兮蘋中,
罾何为兮木上?

Why the birds roost, o at weedy sea?
Why the net spreads, o atop the tree?

沅有茝兮醴有兰,
思公子兮未敢言;

Angelica in Yuan o orchids in Li;
I'm burning for you, o it worries me.

荒忽兮远望,
观流水兮潺湲;

I gaze afar o in trance;
The Yuan gurgles there, o there I glance.

---

*orchid: any of nearly 1,000 genera and more than 25,000 species of attractively flowered plants distributed throughout the world, especially in wet tropics.
*Li: the Li River, the largest river in present-day Hunan Province, a main branch of the Long River. It originates from Mt. Ocean in Guangxi and flows into Lake Miles and Lake Cavehall, more than 800 kilometers long.
*Yuan: the Yuan River, which flows from Longing (Sizhou) in modern Guizhou northeastward to Lake Cavehall in today's Hunan Province.

麋何食兮庭中，

蛟何为兮水裔；

Why the giant elks graze o in the hall?
Why the krakens dwell o a pond small?

朝驰余马兮江皋，

夕济兮西澨；

At dawn my horse gallops o on the bank;
At eve West Shore o hears it clank.

闻佳人兮召余，

将腾驾兮偕逝；

I hear the lady o there call me;
I'd jump up with her o in much glee.

*elk: a large bull-size deer originally of Asia (genus *Alces*), with palmated antlers and the upper lip forming a proboscis for browsing upon trees, commonly known as four-unlikes, which means "having a horse's head but unlike a horse, having a deer's antlers but unlike a deer, having a camel's neck but unlike a camel and having a donkey's tail unlike a donkey".
*kraken: a legendary sea monster, similar to a dragon or a giant octopus.

九歌

筑室兮水中,
葺之兮荷盖;

In water, o a tower's built;
The roof thatched, o lotus tilt.

荪壁兮紫坛,
播芳椒兮成堂;

Cowry steps, o bulrush wall;
Pepper aroma o fills the hall.

桂栋兮兰橑,
辛夷楣兮药房;

Laurel beam, o orchid pole;
Magnolia lintel o scented whole.

---

*lotus: one of the various plants of the waterlily family, noted for their large floating leaves and showy flowers, known as the gentleman's flower because it grows out from the mud, pure and unstained.
*bulrush: a tall, rush-like plant growing in damp ground or water, such as the tall sedge.
*laurel: *laurus nobilis*, a small evergreen tree or shrub with aromatic, lance-shaped leaves, yellowish flowers, and small succulent, cherry-like black fruit, a symbol of glory usually in the form of a crown or wreath of laurel to indicate honor or high merit.

罔薜荔兮为帷,

擗蕙櫋兮既张;

With climbing figs a tent o she does weave;
For the dome fragrant grass o she does cleave.

白玉兮为镇,

疏石兰兮为芳;

White jade placed, o a mat weight;
Pyrrosia laid out, o it smells great.

芷葺兮荷屋,

缭之兮杜衡;

Angelica, o for bowers fair;
Asarum scent o lingers there.

合百草兮实庭,

建芳馨兮庑门;

All herbs in the hall o smell so good;
All flowers by the door o please the mood.

---

*pyrrosia: a fern genus belonging to the family *Polypodiaceae*, which, together with its sister genus *Platycerium*, is better known as the staghorn fern.
*angelica: an aromatic plant belonging to the genus *Angelica*, of the parsley family, cultivated for its aromatic odor and medicinal root and for its stalks that can be candied and eaten.
*asarum: wild ginger, whose beauty lies in its small, jug-shaped flowers and heart-shaped leaves, which in some species are dark green, shiny and mottled with cream.

九 歌

绘画：沈子琪

九嶷缤兮并迎,

灵之来兮如云;

Nine Doubts gods hustle o to and fro,
And spirits like clouds o come and go.

捐余袂兮江中,

遗余褋兮醴浦;

I throw my sachet o to the pour,
And fling my garment o to the shore.

搴汀洲兮杜若,

将以遗兮远者;

On the shoal I pick o pollia grass;
And will send it off o to my lass.

时不可兮骤得,

聊逍遥兮容与!

Opportunities o will not shower;
Why not be patient o for the hour?

---

*Nine Doubts: Mt. Nine Doubts, the mountain where Hibiscus was buried. It was so named because it might confuse people with many of its similar peaks and landscape.
*pollia: an aromatic perennial herb native to China, usually a symbol of purity and integrity.

大司命

Life God Senior

九歌

广开兮天门,

纷吾乘兮玄云;

Wide open, o Heaven's door,
To the hazy clouds, o I will soar.

令飘风兮先驱,

使涷雨兮洒尘;

I bid the wind o to sweep the way,
And ask the storm o the dust to spray.

君回翔兮以下,

逾空桑兮从女;

From the sky you whirl, o you descend;
Through Mt. Mulberry o we now wend.

---

*Life God Senior: God in charge of people's life and death.
*Heaven's Door: any of the four entrances to Heaven in Chinese mythology, that is, East Heaven's Door, West Heaven's Door, South Heaven's Door and North Heaven's Door.
*Mt. Mulberry: There are two mountains called by this name, the former in modern Sha'anxi and the latter in modern Hebei and Shandong.

纷总总兮九州,

何寿夭兮在予;

Hustle and bustle o on the land;
Everybody's life, o in my hand.

高飞兮安翔,

乘清气兮御阴阳。

I soar with ease o on high;
And command Shade and Shine o in airs spry.

吾与君兮齐速,

导帝之兮九坑。

I follow you fast o with respect
And bring God to Nine Mounds o so direct.

---

*Shade and Shine: the most important and basic concept of Chinese or Eastern philosophy or logic, characterized by three features: identification, opposition and interconversion, although apparently standing for two poles of binary opposition, which is what determines human cognition and thought.
*God: God the Lord, the One, Supreme Being, ever-existing and eternal; the infinite creator, sustainer and ruler of the cosmos with the attributes of being omniscient, omnipotent and omnipresent, or else called Father in Heaven or with a natural propensity, the Word, the One, Heaven and so on.
*Nine Mounds: Mt. Nine Mounds. There are two mounts bearing this name in modern Hunan Province. It is not known which one is mentioned here.

九歌

灵衣兮被被，

玉佩兮陆离；

The ghost's costume o does sway;
The jade pendant o does ray.

一阴兮一阳，

众莫知兮余所为；

Shade and Shine, o they combine;
They don't know my act, o they don't know mine.

折疏麻兮瑶华，

将以遗兮离居；

I pick a hemp flower o to impart
To you the spirit o to depart.

---

*hemp: a tall annual Asian herb (*Gannabis sativa*) of the mulberry family, with small green flowers and a tough bark, the fibers from which are used for cloth and cordage.

老冉冉兮既极,

不浸近兮愈疏;

Step by step, old age o gets so near;
One will be estranged, o if not dear.

乘龙兮辚辚,

高驰兮冲天。

Rattle, rattle, o the cart;
To clouds it starts o to dart.

结桂枝兮延伫,

羌愈思兮愁人;

Long, long I stand o with laurel sprays;
The more I yearn, o the more care weighs.

愁人兮奈何,

愿若今兮无亏;

What can I do o with care?
No bad health like today, o ne'er e'er.

---

*laurel: a small evergreen tree that has shiny leaves and yellow or white small flowers and small black fruit, cherished as a symbol of honor.

固人命兮有当，

孰离合兮可为？

Decided by fate, o one's life span;
Who can change the law, o whoe'er can?

绘画：沈子琪

少司命

Life God Junior

秋兰兮麋芜,

罗生兮堂下。

Orchid, lovage, o aligned,
Grow neath the hall, o you find.

绿叶兮素华,

芳菲菲兮袭予。

Green leaves, white flowers, o you see,
With their subtle fragrance, o strike me.

---

*Life God Junior: God in charge of reproduction, especially that of the posterity of humans.
*orchid: any of a widely distributed family of terrestrial or epiphytic monocotyledonous plants having thickened bulbous roots and often very showy distinctive flowers.
*lovage: a selinea-like herb, cultivated as a sweet herb, and for the use in herbal medicine of its root, and to a less degree, the leaves and seeds.

夫人自有兮美子，
荪何以兮愁苦！

They all have daughters and sons o so fair;
Why is the calamus worn o with care?

秋兰兮青青，
绿叶兮紫茎。

Autumn orchids, o green gems;
They have lush leaves, o mauve stems.

满堂兮美人，
忽独与余兮目成。

The hall is filled, o filled so;
But you ogle to me, o your eyes glow.

入不言兮出不辞，
乘回风兮载云旗。

Silently you come, o mutely you go;
Away from me like wind, o a flags flow.

---

*calamus: a semi-evergreen, perennial, hairless herb found in damp, swampy areas, having bright-green sword-shaped leaves with a waxy margin that thicken in the middle.

悲莫悲兮生别离，

乐莫乐兮新相知。

九歌

Sad, very sad, comes the hour o we part;
Glad, very glad, I'll meet mine, o sweet heart.

荷衣兮蕙带，

儵而来兮忽而逝。

Lotus coat, o basil sash,
You rush in and depart o in a flash.

夕宿兮帝郊，

君谁须兮云之际？

In the suburbs o this eve,
Who do you crave mid clouds? O there you cleave.

---

*lotus: an aquatic plant, one of the varieties of the waterlily family, noted for their large floating round leaves and showy flowers, pink or white, a symbol of purity and elegance in Chinese culture: unsoiled though out of soil, so clean with all leaves green.
*basil: a flavorful, leafy green herb of the family *Lamiaceae*, which originated in Asia and Africa, also known as sweet basil or tulsi.

与女沐兮咸池，
晞女发兮阳之阿。

I'd bathe with you o in Cord Pool there;
Shall we in the dale sun o air our hair?

望美人兮未来，
临风怳兮浩歌。

But you do not come, o where's your glance?
I sing to the wind o in a trance.

孔盖兮翠旍，
登九天兮抚彗星。

Emerald flags, o plumed hood,
I'd fly high to sweep comets, o I would.

竦长剑兮拥幼艾，
荪独宜兮为民正。

Sword raised, you hold the kid o in your arms;
You're the best to guard folks o against harm.

---

*Cord Pool: a pool where the sun takes bathes in Chinese mythology, which may be today's Heaven Pool in Mt. Heaven in New Land (the Xinjiang Uighur Autonomous Region); name of a triad of stars in the constellation Celestial Pier.
*comet: a small body orbiting the sun with a substantial fraction of its composition made up of volatile ices, a monstrous star, signifying calamity.

东君

East Lord

九歌

暾将出兮东方,

照吾槛兮扶桑。

East there will rise the sun, o so red,
On my mulberry rails o light shed.

---

*East Lord: what is equivalent to Apollo in western mythology, known as Sun God, who is justice, reason and harmony personified. According to *Rites of Zhou*, a king, i.e. the Son of Heaven does obeisance to Sun God outside the eastern gate of his capital.
*mulberry: the edible, berry-like fruit of a tree (genus *Morus*) whose leaves are valued for sericulture (silkworm farming), and the tree itself, first cultivated in the drainage area of the Yellow River in China about five thousand years ago, a recurring image in traditional Chinese literature.

抚余马兮安驱，

夜皎皎兮既明。

I pat my horse to go, o slow, light;
The night, moonlit, dims, o dawn bright.

驾龙辀兮乘雷，

载云旗兮委蛇。

The rumbling cart I drive o to go;
A wind soughs everywhere, o flags flow.

长太息兮将上，

心低徊兮顾怀。

I will ascend the sky, o a sigh;
I look back and there cast o my eye.

羌声色兮娱人，

观者憺兮忘归。

Pleased with the glamor, o there we roam;
The viewers have forgot o to go home.

---

*horse: a solid four-legged and hoofed herbivorous mammal of the family *Equidae*, widely distributed in the world. It comprises a single species, *Equus caballus*, whose numerous varieties are called breeds. Before the advent of mechanized vehicles, the horse was widely used as a draft animal, and riding on horseback was one of the chief means of transportation.

九歌

緪瑟兮交鼓，

萧钟兮瑶簴。

The drums sound loud, o strings strung;
The bells toll fast, o frame swung.

鸣篪兮吹竽，

思灵保兮贤姱。

Pipes and reeds o played in tune,
With the fair wizard o I'd commune.

翾飞兮翠曾，

展诗兮会舞。

They flit and fly, o rejoice;
They dance and sing, o one voice.

应律兮合节，

灵之来兮敝日。

They dance well o on the beat;
Like clouds come the gods o we'd fain greet.

---

*reed: a musical instrument consisting of thirty-six reeds of different lengths, bound together to form a collection that makes a wind.

青云衣兮白霓裳，

举长矢兮射天狼。

The costumes much like black clouds, o skirt white,
Bows raised, Sirius we will shoot, o we fight.

操余弧兮反沦降，

援北斗兮酌桂浆。

I ply my bow and westward o I sink;
With a ladle I scoop wine o to drink.

撰余辔兮高驰翔，

杳冥冥兮以东行。

I gallop high and high, o I hold my rein,
In darkness rushing o to East Domain.

*Sirius: the Dog Star, Alpha in the constellation of Canis Major, which is used as a metaphor for a villain or a marauder.
*East Domain: the place where the sun puts up for the night before rising the next day.

绘画：沈子琪

河伯

River God

与女游兮九河,

冲风起兮水扬波。

With you I swim now o in the Nine;
The wind raises waves, o ripples fine.

乘水车兮荷盖,

驾两龙兮骖螭。

Lo, the watercart, o lotus hood,
Pulled by dragons, krakens, o so good.

---

*River God: God of the Yellow River. As is said, Fastbow, Fengyi if transliterated, drowned in the Yellow River in the eighth moon, was made River God by God of Heaven.
*the Nine: the Nine Rivers, i.e. the Yellow River, which had nine main branches in ancient China.
*watercart: a kind of warship, also called tower ship, or a metaphor for a big wave or waves.
*dragon: a mythical monster generally represented as a huge winged reptile with a crested head, sharp claws, scaly skin, often spouting fire, flying in rain and living in abysses. It has been worshiped as a reincarnation of divine kingship and a totem of the Chinese nation and all Chinese overseas.
*kraken: a legendary sea monster of northern seas, looking like something between a dragon and an octopus.

登昆仑兮四望，
心飞扬兮浩荡。

九歌

We climb Mt. Queen to gaze, o all parts;
The vista broad does please o our hearts.

日将暮兮怅忘归，
惟极浦兮寤怀。

It's dark and I forget o to return;
Awake, for my land o I more yearn.

鱼鳞屋兮龙堂，
紫贝阙兮珠宫。

The roofs of fish scales, o painted wall;
The gates of mauve shells, o impearled hall.

---

*Mt. Queen: Mt. Kunlun if transliterated, the most sacred mountain in China. It starts from the eastern Pamir Plateau, stretches across New Land (Xinjiang) and Tibet, and extends to Blue Sea (Qinghai), with an average altitude of 5,500-6000 meters. In Chinese myths, Mt. Queen is where Mother West dwells. And Mother West is a sovereign goddess.

灵何为兮水中？

When do you in water o abide?

乘白鼋兮逐文鱼，

与女游兮河之渚；

To seek red carp, a turtle o I do ride;
With you I swim by the shoal, o riverside.

流澌纷兮将来下。

I will follow you close o with floe tide.

---

*carp: fresh water food fish (*Ciprinus carpiao*), originally of China, now widely distributed in Europe and America, a mascot in Chinese culture, symbolizing great success and harmony. An idiom "a carp jumping over the Dragon Gate" means climbing up the social ladder or succeeding in the imperial civil service examination.

*turtle: any of a large and widely distributed order of terrestrial or aquatic reptiles having a toothless beak and a soft body encased in a tough shell into which the head, tail and four legs may be withdrawn. And it is a tortoise-like beast in Chinese mythology, which is said to be a figure of the sixth son of the dragon, and on whose back tablets of great importance are usually carried.

102

九歌

子交手兮东行，
送美人兮南浦。

Let's go to East Sea o hand in hand,
Up to the north shore, o'cross the land.

波滔滔兮来迎，
鱼鳞鳞兮媵予。

The waves surge along o to greet us;
The fish swarm around, o millions plus.

---

*East Sea: a sea of the Pacific Ocean, starting from East China to Korean Peninsula, Kyushu, and the Ryukyu islands on the border, more than 700,000 square kilometers.

山鬼

Mountain Ghost

若有人兮山之阿，

被薛荔兮带女萝。

There seems to be one o on the hill there;
Climbing fig you don, o usnea you wear!

既含睇兮又宜笑，

子慕予兮善窈窕。

With love through your eyes, o you beam to smile;
You say you love me, o me you beguile.

---

*Mountain Ghost: a goddess or a female ghost, supposed to be a fantastic spirit of woods or stones, a fairy-like beautiful sprite or manito capable of romancing: loving and love-making.
*climbing fig: pomelo fig, an evergreen vine with egg-shaped thick leaves two or three inches long, blowing small flowers and bearing fig-like fruit.
*usnea: a parasitic herb with vines and tendrils winding around an uptight tree trunk or branch to support itself, also known as beard lichen, tree's dandruff, woman's long hair, or tree moss, old man's beard, beard moss, having been used in traditional Chinese medicine for over 2,000 years.

乘赤豹兮从文狸，

辛夷车兮结桂旗。

九歌

A leopard pulls ahead, o a wildcat tags;
Magnolia for the cart, o laurel for flags.

---

*leopard: also called panther, a large strong cat (*Panthera pardus*) of southern Asia and Africa that is adept at climbing and is usually tawny or buff with black spots arranged in rosettes, living in forests, mountains, deserts, or grasslands, closely related to the lion, tiger, and jaguar.
*wildcat: any of a large group of fierce, medium-sized undomesticated cats, including the bobcat, lynx, ocelot, serval and so on.
*magnolia: any of numerous evergreen or deciduous trees and shrubs of the genus *Magnolia* of the Western Hemisphere and Asia, having large, showy, often fragrant flowers, white, pink, purple or yellow, and widely cultivated as ornamentals.
*laurel: *Laurus nobilis*, an evergreen shrub, valued for its aromatic, ovate or lance-shaped leaves, yellowish flowers, and succulent, cherry-like fruit, a symbol of glory usually in the form of a crown or wreath of laurel to indicate honor or high merit.

被石兰兮带杜衡,

折芳馨兮遗所思。

Pyrrosia you don, o asarum you wear;
I pick you fragrant flowers, o my lady fair.

余处幽篁兮终不见天,

路险难兮独后来。

In the recesses of bamboo, o it's dim all day;
I have come so late, o it's a hard way.

表独立兮山之上,

云容容兮而在下。

Atop the mountain o I stand alone;
Below my two feet o white clouds are blown.

*pyrrosia: a fern genus belonging to the family *Polypodiaceae*, which, together with its sister genus *Platycerium*, better known as the staghorn fern.
*asarum: any of a wide range of species of evergreen, low-growing, and rhizomatous woodland perennials.
*bamboo: a tall, tree-like or shrubby evergreen grass in tropical and semi-tropical regions, a symbol of integrity and altitude in Chinese culture.

杳冥冥兮羌昼晦，
东风飘兮神灵雨。

九歌

So dim and so dark, o just like the night;
East wind soughs and soughs, o a rain so light.

留灵修兮憺忘归，
岁既晏兮孰华予。

I'm so enamoured, o please do not go;
The year is o'er now, o will my flower blow?

采三秀兮于山间，
石磊磊兮葛蔓蔓。

Ganoderma I pick o on the hill;
Rugged, rugged boulders, o kudzus fill.

---

*ganoderma: *Ganoderma Lucidum Karst* in Latin, a grass with an umbrella top, a pore fungus, used as medicine and tonic in China.
*kudzu: an extremely fast-growing, climbing and trailing perennial vine. The plant can develop an extensive and deep root system, and over time, produce massive tubers. The stems are herbaceous and hairy when young, becoming fibrous to woody with age, and can grow to 100 feet long and the leaves are alternately arranged, trifoliate.

怨公子兮怅忘归,

君思我兮不得闲。

So gloomy, I stay, o engaged you'd be;
You miss me, don't you? O you can't be free.

山中人兮芳杜若,

饮石泉兮荫松柏。

You loom in the hills, o a pollia fine;
I drink the stone spring o beneath the pine.

---

*pollia: a perennial herb with actinomorphic flowers and free, shallowly boat-shaped sepals and baccate, globose fruit.
*pine: any of a genus (*Pinus*) of evergreen trees of the pine family, a cone-bearing tree having bundles of two to five needle-shaped leaves growing in clusters, an important image in Chinese literature, a symbol of rectitude, longevity and so on.
*monkey: any of a group of primates usually having a flat, hairless face, elongate limbs, hands and feet adapted for grasping, and a highly developed nervous system, including marmosets, baboons, and macaques, but not the anthropoid apes, though monkeys and apes are used alternatively in Chinese, also used as a metaphor for somebody who is mischievous and shrewdly calculating.
*ape: a large, tailless or long-tail primate, as a gorilla or chimpanzee, loosely any monkey, often referring to monkeys.

108

九歌

君思我兮然疑作,

Do you really yearn? O in doubt I burn.

雷填填兮雨冥冥,
猿啾啾兮狖夜鸣。

The thunder rumbles, o the rain's like haze;
The monkey mumbles, o the ape loud bays.

风飒飒兮木萧萧,
思公子兮徒离忧。

The wind soughs and soughs, o there swish the leaves;
I miss you, lady, o my poor heart grieves.

国殇

The Death of the State

九歌

操吴戈兮被犀甲，

车错毂兮短兵接。

Wu spears held in hand, o in rhino mails,
The soldiers combat, o crossed chariot trails.

旌蔽日兮敌若云，

矢交坠兮士争先。

Enemy like clouds, o flags shade the sun;
Through falling arrows, o all fighters run.

---

*Wu: the State of Wu (12th century B.C.-473 B.C.), founded by Great One and Use Two, King Civil of Zhou's two elder uncles in the lower reaches of the Long River before the founding of Zhou, ratified as a vassal state by King Martial of Zhou, annexed by the State of Yue (2032 B.C.-222 B.C.) in the end.
*Wu spear: a spear made in Wu, usually the best quality spear made of bronze, as famous as Yue sword in Chinese history.
*rhino: a large herbivorous, odd-toed mammal of Africa and Asia, with one or two keratin-fiber horns on the snout, a very thick hide, and the upper lip protruded and prehensile.

凌余阵兮躐余行,

左骖殪兮右刃伤。

Dashing on our front, o our lines they tread;
The right steeds are stabbed, o the left fall, dead.

霾两轮兮絷四马,

援玉枹兮击鸣鼓。

The wheels are sunken o horse feet are tied;
The drums are beaten, o drumsticks are plied.

天时怼兮威灵怒,

严杀尽兮弃原野。

The gods all complain, o furious the sky;
The soldiers lie waste, o wounded to die.

出不入兮往不反,

平原忽兮路超远。

Out they go, not back, o no living souls;
The way stretches far, o the wildness rolls.

*steed: a horse; especially a spirited war horse. The use of horses in war can be traced back to the Shang dynasty (1600 B.C.-1046 B.C.), when a department of horse management was established. A verse from *the Book of Songs* tells of Lord Civil of Watch's industriousness: "In state affairs he leads; / He has three thou-sand steeds."

九歌

带长剑兮挟秦弓，
首身离兮心不惩。

They carry long swords, o with bows of Qin,
Head cut off the trunk, o their heart kept in.

诚既勇兮又以武，
终刚强兮不可凌。

Courageous they are, o brimming with pride;
Unyielding they are, o not to o'erride.

身既死兮神以灵，
魂魄毅兮为鬼雄。

Although they are dead, o their souls live on;
Even they are ghosts, o they're ghosts best done.

---

*Qin: the State of Qin (905 B.C.-206 B.C.), a fief allotted by King Piety of Zhou to Fei Ying or (Feizi Ying), the progeny of Brim One (Yi One), which later became one of the most powerful vassal states in Warring State period and developed into the first unified regime of China, i.e. the Qin Empire.
*ghost best done: referring to a martyr, the best in the netherworld.

礼魂

Soul of the Rite

成礼兮会鼓,

传芭兮代舞,

The rite o'er, o the drums pound;
Now they dance, o flowers around.

姱女倡兮容与。

The belle sings loud, o a mellow sound.

春兰兮秋菊,

长无绝兮终古。

Spring orchid, o autumn mum,
They last long for ages o to come.

---

*the rite: referring to the ceremony of a sacrifice offered to gods.
*spring orchid: orchid, a symbol of elegance, used for bouquets in spring when homage is paid.
*autumn mum: chrysanthemum, a symbol of rectitude and longevity, used for bouquets in autumn, especially when homage is paid.

九章 | Nine Cantos

惜诵

九章

O Remonstration

惜诵以致愍兮,
发愤以抒情。

O my remonstration caused a bane;
In wrath, I now let out my pain.

所作忠而言之兮,
指苍天以为正。

O if I'm not out of fealty expressed;
The Heavens above can be my test.

---

*Heavens: the distant sky of the sun, moon, and stars, the abode of God who is the superintendent of the human world, and also the abode of the blessed dead.

令五帝以折中兮,

戒六神与向服。

O Five Sovereigns can be my judge good;
To Six Gods I'd make it plain, I would.

俾山川以备御兮,

命咎繇使听直。

O mountain and river gods, come along;
Judge, Your Honor, try what's right or wrong.

竭忠诚以事君兮,

反离群而赘肬。

O I have served our liege lord heart and soul;
They despise me as a surplus role.

---

*Five Sovereigns: the five saintly leaders of Allied Nations in prehistoric China before the founding of the Xia dynasty, that is, Great Sky (Taihao) in the east, Fire God (Yandi) in the south, Young Sky (Shaohao) in the west, Plump Head (Zhuanxu) in the north, and Lord Yellow (Huangdi) in the middle.
*Six Gods: the gods in charge of natural phenomena: God of Cold, God of Heat; God of the Sun, God of the Moon, God of Stars and God of Drought.
*Judge: alias Moor Potter (cir. 2,219 B.C.-2,113 B.C.), Gaoyao if transliterated, a law enforcer under Mound, an important statesman, thinker, educator and lawyer in prehistoric China, one of the Four Saints in Old China, the other three being Mound, Hibiscus, and Worm.

九章

忘儇媚以背众兮,
待明君其知之。

O I've vexed them all, a fawner I'm not;
May our sagacious lord know the lot.

言与行其可迹兮,
情与貌其不变。

O all my words and deeds you can well trace;
I've never ever changed, heart or face.

故相臣莫若君兮,
所以证之不远。

O with our lord no subject can compare;
The proof is before our eyes, just there.

吾谊先君而后身兮,
羌众人之所仇也。

O I present our lord first and myself then,
But I'm so resented by all those men.

专惟君而无他兮,

又众兆之所雠也。

O lord, my heart holds no others but you,
But the crowd all regard me as a foe.

壹心而不豫兮,

羌不可保也。

O I stand so staunch, I ne'er suspect,
But I cannot myself protect.

疾亲君而无他兮,

有招祸之道也。

O I try to serve our lord, nothing more,
But this leads to a bane, to a sore.

思君其莫我忠兮,

忽忘身之贱贫。

O lord, nobody's more faithful than me,
But I forget a poor man I be.

事君而不贰兮,

迷不知宠之门。

O I have served my lord with one mind,
Ne'er to curry favor, ne'er that kind.

九章

忠何罪以遇罚兮,

亦非余心之所志。

O although faithful, I'm punished like that;
It's what I've ne'er thought of, ne'er driven at.

行不群以巅越兮,

又众兆之所咍。

O incongruent with the crowd, I'm capsized;
And I am by the swarm satirized.

纷逢尤以离谤兮,

謇不可释也。

O that blame, that slander I can't prevent;
That great agony I can't vent.

情沉抑而不达兮,

又蔽而莫之白也。

O the depression I can't express, ne'er;
And the deception I cannot lay bare.

心郁邑余侘傺兮,

又莫察余之中情。

O my dire melancholy, my dire glum!
Who understands me, who can this o'ercome?

固烦言不可结诒兮,

愿陈志而无路。

O my endless words I have no way to send;
I'd tell my will, but no way to wend.

退静默而莫余知兮,

进号呼又莫吾闻。

O I would withdraw, but this none knows about;
I would advance, but none can hear my shout.

申侘傺之烦惑兮,

中闷瞀之忳忳。

O all frustration brings about distress;
My skein of sorrow I can't express.

昔余梦登天兮,

魂中道而无杭。

O once, I dreamed of surfing the sky;
Stopped by a stream, I'd no boat to ply.

九章

吾使厉神占之兮,
曰:"有志极而无旁。"

O I've asked a sorcerer to divine;
He replied: "You've a great will, but no comrade fine."

终危独以离异兮,
曰君可思而不可恃。

"O would I be so estranged in the end?"
He replied: "A lord you can serve; on him you can't depend."

故众口其铄金兮,
初若是而逢殆。

O many mouths can melt a tael of gold;
You incur danger because you're bold.

惩於羹者而吹齑兮,
何不变此志也?

O those who are scalded e'en cool a dish cold;
Why do you still to your will fast hold?

欲释阶而登天兮，

犹有曩之态也。

O with no ladder, to the sky you'd soar;
You have never changed, just like before.

众骇遽以离心兮，

又何以为此伴也？

O with you the crowd do not share a heart;
Why will they in helping you play a part?

同极而异路兮，

又何以为此援也？

O you're different despite the same lord,
Howe'er, why do they help you in accord?

晋申生之孝子兮，

父信谗而不好。

九章

O Outbirth in Chin was a filial son;
Hoodwinked, his father killed him anon.

行婞直而不豫兮，

鲧功用而不就。

O Great Fish was so staunch and so upright;
He could not achieve what he aimed right.

---

*Outbirth: Outbirth (?-656 B.C.), Shensheng if transliterated, a crown prince of Chin in the Spring and Autumn period, who hanged himself, having been framed and persecuted by Lady Steed, his father's wife, a beautiful cunning lady.
*Jin: the State of Jin (1033 B.C.-376 B.C.), a vassal state under Suzerain Zhou. In the last stage of the Spring and Autumn period, the State of Jin waned and was controlled by six lords. After tangled warfare among the six lords, three remained (Zhao, Way, Han) and finally partitioned Chin into three different states, which was a representative watershed of the Spring and Autumn period and the Waring States period.
*Great Fish: Kun if transliterated, father of Great Worm, the First King of Xia (21 Century B.C.-16 Century B.C.), a forerunner of water conservation in Chinese culture.

吾闻作忠以造怨兮,

忽谓之过言。

O I hear loyalty might hatred incur;
I don't care, as a gauge may err.

九折臂而成医兮,

吾至今而知其信然。

O hurt nine times, one'd be a doctor too,
Now I have come to understand it is so true.

矰弋机而在上兮,

罻罗张而在下。

O all arrows fly above through the air,
And below you find a trap or snare.

设张辟以娱君兮,

愿侧身而无所。

O all the machinery for our lord!
Where'er can I find a standing board?

欲儃徊以干傺兮,

恐重患而离尤。

O I linger, and to our lord I'd cling;
I fear a curse will fall from a sling.

欲高飞而远集兮，

君罔谓女何之。

O I would fly high and fly far away;
Our king may say "Why this you betray?"

欲横奔而失路兮，

坚志而不忍。

O just like those flunkies, I would now flee;
So staunch, hardhearted I can't be.

背膺牉以交痛兮，

心郁结而纡轸。

O my, I'll be torn and rent, chest and back;
Sadness pent up, what a pain, alack!

梼木兰以矫蕙兮,

鑿申椒以为粮。

O for eupatories, basil I'll pound;
For dried food, I'll have Shen pepper ground.

播江离与滋菊兮,

愿春日以为糗芳。

O selinea 'n chrysanthemums I'll sow;
In spring they'll be my food, I expect so.

---

*eupatory: an aromatic herb, looking like arethusa, growing by waterside, with purple stems, red at protuberant joints, four to five feet tall, with glossy leaves which are long, pointed at end and saw-toothed on edges, luxuriant in summer.
*Shen pepper: *Zanthoxylum bungeanum*, Chinese prickly ash, an aromatic ash tree bearing seeds used as a spice, native to the State of Shen, an ancient state contemporary with Shang and Zhou.
*basil: also known as sweet basil or tulsi, a tender low-growing herb that is grown as a perennial in warm, tropical climates. Basil is originally native to India and other tropical regions of Asia. It has been cultivated there for more than 5,000 years.
*selinea: an aromatic medicinal herb, an umbelliferous plant one to two feet tall, often used as decorations.
*chrysanthemum: any of a genus of about 40 species of flowering plants in the aster family, native primarily to subtropical and temperate areas, a perennial (*Chryanthemum*) of the composite family, some cultivated varieties of which have large heads of showy flowers of various colors, a symbol of purity or longevity in Chinese culture.

恐情质之不信兮,

故重著以自明。

九章

O I fear my faith I can't well explain;
So I'm expressed again and again.

矫兹媚以私处兮,

愿曾思而远身。

O to keep my worth I would go away;
I've thought if I could in quietude stay.

沈子琪

涉江

Crossing the River

九章

余幼好此奇服兮,
年既老而不衰。

O since young I've loved clothes strange, a queer mould;
I haven't declined e'en though now old.

带长铗之陆离兮,
冠切云之崔嵬,

O a long sword I carry on my waist
And I wear a crown so highly raised,

被明月兮佩宝璐。

With Luna inlaid, o with the best jade.

---

*Luna: the moon, an important image in Chinese literature or culture as it can give rise to many associations such as solitude and nostalgia on the one hand, and purity, brightness and happy reunions on the other. What is "moon" in Chinese has at least two hundred names by analogy, like Jade Mound (yaotai), Fair Lady (chanjuan), Jade Hare (Yutu), White Hare (baitu), Silver Hare (yintu), Ice Hare (bingtu), Gold Hare (jintu), Hare Gleam (tuhui), Laurel Soul (Guipo) and so on.

世混浊而莫余知兮,

吾方高驰而不顾。

O the turbid world does not understand me;
Now I would gallop high, of all care free.

驾青虬兮骖白螭,

吾与重华游兮瑶之圃。

Astride a dragon blue, o a dragon white,
With Lord Mound o I will tour Lord Heaven's park jade bright.

---

*dragon: a fabulous giant serpent-like winged animal that can change its girth and length, often flying in rain and living in abysses, a symbol of benevolence and sovereignty in Chinese culture, a totem of the Chinese nation, a totem of all Chinese across the world.
*Lord Mound: Mound (2,377 B.C.-2,259 B.C.), Yao if transliterated, a descendant of Lord Yellow, enfeoffed with Qi at 13 years old and founding his capital at Taotang (or Tang) at 15. Divine and noble, Mound has been regarded as one of Five Lords in ancient China, the initiator of the demise of the throne in Chinese history.

登昆仑兮食玉英，
与天地兮同寿，
与日月兮同光。

九章

Mt. Queen I'll climb, o on jade flowers I'll dine;
I'll live long o with Heaven and earth;
With the sun and the moon, o I'll shine.

哀南夷之莫吾知兮，
旦余济乎江湘。

O woe, the native southerners don't me know;
I cross the river when the cocks crow.

乘鄂渚而反顾兮，
欸秋冬之绪风。

O on O Shoal I look back to behold;
The slash of wintry wind soughs, so cold.

---

*Mt. Queen: or Mt. Kunlun if transliterated, the most sacred mountain in China. It starts from the Eastern Pamir Plateau, stretches across New Land (XinJiang if transliterated) and Tibet, and extends to Blue Sea (Qinghai), with an average altitude of 5,500-6,000 meters. In Chinese myths, Mt. Queen is where Mother West dwells.
*jade flowers: said to be eaten by fairies to give them immortality.
*O Shoal: a shoal in the Long River, east of present-day Mightboom (Wuchang), Wuhan, Hubei Province.

绘画：沈子琪

九章

步余马兮山皋，
邸余车兮方林。

The hill marsh o I let my horse rove,
And stop my cart o beside the grove.

乘舲船余上沅兮，
齐吴榜以击汰。

O on the Yuan River I ride my yacht;
My oar I ply and the waves I swat.

船容与而不进兮，
淹回水而疑滞。

O my boat behind the waves can't advance,
Stuck by the whirlpools that seem to dance.

---

*the Yuan River: an important river in today's Hunan Province, starting from Guizhou and flowing into Lake Cavehall.

朝发枉渚兮，

夕宿辰阳。

O at dawn Bent Shoal I leave,
And reach Starshine at eve.

苟余心其端直兮，

虽僻远之何伤。

O if my heart is kind, so fair and square;
Why should I the remote distance care?

入溆浦余儃徊兮，

迷不知吾所如。

O I feel at a loss at Shoreside Shoal;
Where shall I go now? What a lost soul!

---

*Bent Shoal: south of today's Ever Virtue (Changde), Hunan Province.
*Starshine: in Poolbent (Tanwan) west of today's Starstream (Chenxi) County, Hunan Province.
*Shoreside Shoal: in the River Shore, a river in today's Hunan flowing into the River Yuan.

九章

深林杳以冥冥兮，
乃猿狖之所居。

O deep the woods, where Hades does preside,
A place where macaques and apes abide.

山峻高以蔽日兮，
下幽晦以多雨。

O the mountains, so steep, shade the sun;
It's dark below and a rain soughs on.

霰雪纷其无垠兮，
云霏霏而承宇。

O the graupel whirls and whirls without bound;
Shrouding the sky and dimming the ground.

---

*Hades: the abode of the dead, and a euphemism for hell.
*macaque: a monkey with a stout body, short tail, cheek pouches, and pronounced muzzle.
*ape: a large, tailless primate, as a gorilla or chimpanzee, loosely any monkey.

哀吾生之无乐兮,

幽独处乎山中。

O my unhappy wretched life I mourn,
Living in the mountains, so forlorn.

吾不能变心而从俗兮,

固将愁苦而终穷。

O I can't follow the vulgar, I won't change my mind;
I shall end my life, to distress confined.

接舆髡首兮,

桑扈臝行。

O Cartjoiner had hair cut;
Mulberry did nude strut.

忠不必用兮,

贤不必以。

O loyals are not employed;
Sages may be destroyed.

---

*Cartjoiner: a contemporary of Confucius, a hermit known as the "madman of Chu" in King Glare of Chu reign, letting loose his long hair undressed, pretending to be mad, and later having his hair shaven.
*Mulberry: Sir Mulberry Vitex, a famous Wordist and hermit in the Warring States period, said to live or abide naked in defiance against the mainstream canonical values.

伍子逢殃兮,

比干菹醢。

九章

O Clerk Wu was so debased;
Bican was made meat paste.

与前世而皆然兮,

吾又何怨乎今之人!

O now like before it is just the same;
Why should I the people of today blame?

余将董道而不豫兮,

固将重昏而终身!

O I won't hesitate, I'll keep on the strife,
Though I may be in the dark all my life.

---

*Clerk Wu: Clerk Wu (559 B.C.-484 B.C.), a minister and militarist of the State of Wu during the late years of the Spring and Autumn Period, killed for remonstrating his king Fuchai (cir. 528 B.C.-473 B.C.).

*Bican: Bican (1110 B.C.-1047 B.C.), bigan if transliterated, the prime minister of Shang, who had served the court as an imperial tutor since he was 20. He was loyal and caring for the people, usually remonstrated King Chow with blunt words. Bican's admonition finally irritated King Chow and he was martyred, his heart taken out.

乱曰：鸾鸟凤皇，

日以远兮。

The finale says, Roc and Phoenix, o they
Fly afar day by day.

燕雀乌鹊，

巢堂坛兮。

Sparrows and magpies, they
On the altar eggs lay.

---

*Roc: a legendary enormous powerful bird of prey. In Chinese mythology, it was transformed from a fish in North Sea. *Sir Lush*, one of the most important Wordist classics, reads like this: There in North Sea is a fish called Minnow, whose body spans about a thousand miles. When transformed into a bird, it is called Roc, whose back spans about a thousand miles. With a burst of vigor, it flies up, whose wings are like clouds hemming the sky. This bird, skimming tides, flies to South Sea. And this South Sea is called the Pool of Heaven.

*phoenix: a legendary bird of great beauty, unique of its kind, which is supposed to live five or six hundred years before consuming itself by fire, rising again from its ashes to live through another cycle, hence a symbol of immortality. In Chinese mythology, the phoenix only perches on phoenix trees, i.e. firmiana, only eats firmiana fruit, and only drinks sweet spring water, and this mythic bird appears only in times of peace and sagacious rule.

*sparrow: a small, plain-colored passerine bird related to the finches, grosbeaks and buntings, a very common bird in China, a symbol of insignificance.

*magpie: a jaylike passerine corvine bird, having a long and graduated tail and featured with black-and-white coloring, which often makes loud chirps to report good news, as is believed by many Chinese.

露申辛夷,

死林薄兮。

九章

Daphnes and magnolias,
O die in woods and grass.

腥臊并御,

芳不得薄兮。

The stinky get employed;
O the fragrant aren't enjoyed.

---

*daphne: an aromatic herb, also known as the fragrant daphne, any of a genus (*Daphne*) of a showy and fragrant evergreen Eurasian shrubs of the mezereon family with apetalous flowers whose colored calyx resembles a corolla.
*magnolia: any of a genus (*Magnolia*) of trees or shrubs with large, fragrant and usually showy flowers, in this poem referring to *Magnolia liliflora* Desr. , which includes species such as *Magnolia denudata* Desr., *Magnolia sprengerii* Pamp. and *Mognolia biondii* Pamp.

阴阳易位，

时不当兮。

Shade and Shine not in place,
Ill-timed, o what disgrace!

怀信佗傺，

忽乎吾将行兮！

Loyals are cursed instead;
O I'll go forward, I'll go ahead.

---

*Shade and Shine: the most important and basic concept of Chinese or Eastern philosophy, representing the very basic element and force in the universe, characterized by three features: identification, opposition and interconversion, although apparently standing for two poles of binary opposition.

抽思

Thought Reeled Off

九章

心郁郁之忧思兮,
独永叹乎增伤。

O what depression, what a long strain of woe;
My lonely long sigh adds to my rue.

思蹇产之不释兮,
曼遭夜之方长。

O the entangled sadness I can't shear;
The night drags on, so long and so drear.

悲秋风之动容兮,
何回极之浮浮。

O the autumn sough does the plants deface;
Why do Heaven and earth turn apace?

数惟荪之多怒兮，

伤余心之忧忧。

O I think of you who do tend to flare;
So hurt, the pains I can hardly bear.

愿摇起而横奔兮，

览民尤以自镇。

O really I'd leave you and rush away;
But for people's pain, I stop to stay.

结微情以陈词兮，

矫以遗夫美人。

O I'll write into verse what's in heart stored,
And I'll present it to you, my lord.

昔君与我诚言兮，

曰黄昏以为期。

O you made an appointment with me there,
Saying: Evening is the hour to fare.

羌中道而回畔兮，

反既有此他志。

O you did repent your words and withdrew
And got engaged with what you would do.

九章

忳吾以其美好兮,
览余以其修姱。

O to me you put on your beaming face;
To me you displayed your charming grace.

与余言而不信兮,
盖为余而造怒。

O you did betray whate'er you had said;
Why did you get so enraged instead?

愿承閒而自察兮,
心震悼而不敢。

O I would make time to make a clean breast,
But I dare not get myself expressed.

悲夷犹而冀进兮,
心怛伤之憺憺。

O pained, I still want to tell you my woe;
So bitter, I can't express my rue.

兹历情以陈辞兮,

荪详聋而不闻。

O I would explain to you what I fear;
But you would always turn a deaf ear.

固切人之不媚兮,

众果以我为患。

O a just man would not fawn on the lord;
I'm seen by all as a bane, ignored.

初吾所陈之耿著兮,

岂至今其庸亡?

O isn't what I said at the start so clear
That you have forgotten all, sheer?

何独乐斯之謇謇兮?

愿荪美之可光。

O why did I make bold to give you advice?
I wish that your worth would greatly rise.

望三王以为像兮,

指彭咸以为仪。

九章

O I wish Three Kings were your models true
And Cord Peng were your example too.

夫何极而不至兮,

故远闻而难亏。

O what aim could you not fulfill, what aim?
To posterity you'd leave your name.

善不由外来兮,

名不可以虚作。

O goodness you'd practise and conserve;
Your good reputation you'd deserve.

---

*Three Kings: the first kings of the three earliest dynasties in Chinese history, that is, Worm of Xia, Hotspring of Shang and King Civil of Zhou.
*Cord Peng: an upright intellectual and minister in the Shang dynasty, who drowned himself in protest against the state of affairs under the tyrannic rule of King Chow. Our poet, Yuan Qu followed his example.

孰无施而有报兮，

孰不实而有获？

O how could you e'er have lush leaves with roots?
How could you have a fill without fruits?

少歌曰：

To sum up:

与美人抽思兮，

并日夜而无正。

O to the lord I reel off my thought;
Day and night well-treated I'm not.

侨吾以其美好兮，

敖朕辞而不听。

O I praise you are beautiful indeed,
But full of pride, you will never heed.

倡曰：

有鸟自南兮，

来集汉北。

Thus it's Sung:
O a bird from the south flies
To North of Han and cries.

---

*North of Han: the first place where our poet lived in exile, in today's Hubei Province.

148

好姱佳丽兮，

胖独处此异域。

九章

O with bright plumage it's blessed;
So lonely, in this land it does rest.

既惸茕独而不群兮，

又无良媒在其侧。

O so lonely, off the crowd I abide,
And there's no good go-between by my side.

道卓远而日忘兮，

愿自申而不得。

O you leave me forgotten day by day;
I would explain, but you are away.

望北山而流涕兮，

临流水而太息。

O I gaze at North Hill, my tears run dry;
To the running water I long sigh.

---

*North Hill: a hill unidentified in this poem.

望孟夏之短夜兮，

何晦明之若岁？

O a summer night is short, a night mere;
Why is it so long, much like a year?

惟郢路之辽远兮，

魂一夕而九逝。

O is the way to Capital so long?
My dream's been there nine times, wrong, wrong, wrong.

曾不知路之曲直兮，

南指月与列星。

O I don't know wheth'r the road is bent or straight;
I'll rush south to the moon and stars, great!

愿径逝而未得兮，

魂识路之营营。

O I would go, but the way I don't know;
To find the way ghosts run to and fro.

*Capital: referring to Ying, Chu's capital for four hundred years, near today's Chasteton (Jingzhou), Hubei Province.

九章

何灵魂之信直兮，
人之心不与吾心同！

O why is my spirit so fair and square?
But others' heart is not the same as mine, ne'er e'er.

理弱而媒不通兮，
尚不知余之从容。

O go-betweens, weak, can't communicate;
They don't know yet I'm upright and straight.

乱曰：

The finale says,

长濑湍流，
溯江潭兮。

Rapids long, water fast;
I go up, I go past.

狂顾南行，

聊以娱心兮。

A look back, south I go
O to let go of my woe.

轸石崴嵬，

蹇吾愿兮。

My heart's like the rock tall;
I'd fly to Capital.

超回志度，

行隐进兮。

O'er the sheer crag I fly;
On the way people hie.

低徊夷犹，

宿北姑兮。

The roadside stream does purl;
I'll rest there in North Girl.

烦冤瞀容，

实沛徂兮。

I'm upset and perturbed,
Like waterflow uncurbed.

---

*North Girl: a place unidentified in this poem.

绘画：沈子

愁叹苦神,

灵遥思兮。

Now I sigh and I burn;
For the distance I yearn.

路远处幽,

又无行媒兮。

The way's far and remote;
O of me no one takes note.

道思作颂,

聊以自救兮。

I make my woe a verse
O my sadness to disperse.

忧心不遂,

斯言谁告兮。

Care-laden, so unwell,
O to whom can I this tell?

哀郢

Mourning Ying

九章

皇天之不纯命兮,
何百姓之震愆?

O August Heaven, you change, change again;
Why do the folk suffer all the pain?

民离散而相失兮,
方仲春而东迁。

O people get apart, not staid the least;
Right in Moon Two, they flee to the east.

去故乡而就远兮,
遵江夏以流亡。

O having left home, far away they're gone,
Along the rivers that flow, flow on.

---

*Moon Two: the second moon or the second moon of spring according to Chinese Lunar calendar.

出国门而轸怀兮，
甲之鼌吾以行。

O now out of the state's gate, I do mourn,
After I started off at Crust's dawn.

发郢都而去闾兮，
怊荒忽其焉极？

O I've started from Ying, leaving my home;
In a daze and trance, where shall I roam?

楫齐扬以容与兮，
哀见君而不再得。

O I linger in my boat, raised my oar;
Woe, no chance to see my lord, what a sore!

望长楸而太息兮，
涕淫淫其若霰。

O at the catalpa, long long I sigh;
Like graupel, tears roll down from the eye.

---

*Crust: the first day of the first decade of a moon according to Chinese Lunar calendar, meaning the state before grass burgeons to pierce the crust.
*catalpa, a genus (*Catalpa*) of eight species of trees (family *Bignoniaceae*) native to eastern Asia, eastern North America, and the West Indies. The common, or southern, catalpa (C. *bignonioides*), which yields a durable timber, is one of the most widely planted ornamental species.

九章

过夏首而西浮兮,
顾龙门而不见。

O crossing the Summer, I drift west now;
I look back at Ying, it's nowhere, how?

心婵媛而伤怀兮,
眇不知其所蹠。

O I'm so anxious and I'm so obsessed;
Where is my way and where shall I quest?

顺风波以从流兮,
焉洋洋而为客。

O I follow the river with waves in;
A wandering life I now begin.

凌阳侯之氾滥兮,
忽翱翔之焉薄。

O I surf the flood and I surf the pour;
Where shall I roost? Like a bird I soar.

---

*Ying: the capital of the State of Chu for four hundred years, four kilometers north of today's Chaste Town (Jingzhou), Hubei Province.

心绪结而不解兮，

思蹇产而不释。

O the knot in my heart I can't untie;
Worries and cares do me occupy.

将运舟而下浮兮，

上洞庭而下江。

O downstream, downstream I will row my boat;
From Lake Cavehall to the Long I float.

去终古之所居兮，

今逍遥而来东。

O I have left, my hometown far away;
And have drifted to East Land today.

羌灵魂之欲归兮，

何须臾而忘反。

O my soul would go back to the old bower;
Have I forgot it, one day or hour?

---

*Lake Cavehall: a lake cutting across present-day Hunan and Hubei provinces, the second largest freshwater lake in China, famous for its natural resources and cultural heritage.
*the Long River: a grand river originating from the Tanggula Mountains on Tibet Plateau, flowing through 13 provincial areas including the Tibet Autonomous Region, more than 6,300 kilometers long, the longest river in China and the third longest in the world.

九章

背夏浦而西思兮，
哀故都之日远。

O against the Summer westward I yearn;
Our capital's far away I burn!

登大坟以远望兮，
聊以舒吾忧心。

O climbing up the high mound, far I gaze
To drive from my heart the shrouding haze.

哀州土之平乐兮，
悲江介之遗风。

O with the peace of this land I'm obsessed;
With the relics ashore I'm depressed.

当陵阳之焉至兮，
淼南渡之焉如？

O facing Ridge Shine now, where shall I go?
Crossing the river, where shall I row?

---

*Ridge Shine: in today's Green Shine County or south of Peace Blessed (Anqing), Anhui Province.

曾不知夏之为丘兮，

孰两东门之可芜？

O don't you know the mansions now lie waste,
And the two east gates have been erased?

心不怡之长久兮，

忧与愁其相接。

O the displeasure's been with me for long;
My sorrow has been combined with wrong.

惟郢路之辽远兮，

江与夏之不可涉。

O to Ying it's a long long way to go;
In the Long and the Summer I can't row.

忽若去不信兮，

至今九年而不复。

O exiled, I'm not trusted, alack;
For nine years in all I have not been back.

---

*the Summer: the Summer River, a river flowing from the Long River into the Han River in summer, but is dried up in winter, hence so named.

九章

惨郁郁而不通兮，
蹇侘傺而含戚。

O melancholy pent up, I'm not glad;
With tribulations, I feel so sad.

外承欢之汋约兮，
谌荏弱而难持。

O they flatter, all subservience, so meek;
In fact, they are immoral, so weak.

忠湛湛而愿进兮，
妒被离而鄣之。

O loyal and devoted, I'd advance;
But all jealousy, all evil stance.

尧舜之抗行兮，
瞭杳杳而薄天。

O Mound and Hibiscus, noble and high;
So detached, they are close to the sky.

---

*Mound and Hibiscus: two prehistoric sagacious kings in ancient China, having been regarded as models of the best rulers in Chinese history.

众谗人之嫉妒兮,

被以不慈之伪名。

O the slanderers, jealous of the two,
Called them unfilial, as has proved untrue.

憎愠惀之修美兮,

好夫人之慷慨。

O our lord does hate reserved virtuous worth,
But loves what is magnanimous froth.

众踥蹀而日进兮,

美超远而逾迈。

O those who curry favor have their day;
The sages are kept far far away.

乱曰:

The finale says,

曼余目以流观兮,

冀一反之何时。

O I glance and let my sight go around,
And wish to go back, homebound.

鸟飞反故乡兮,

狐死必首丘。

九章

O back to their nest all birds will fly;
Foxes face their home when they die.

信非吾罪而弃逐兮,

何日夜而忘之!

O I've not been exiled because of my crime;
Can I forget my land any time?

---

*fox: a burrowing canine mammal (genus *Vulpes*) having a long pointed muzzle and a long bushy tail, commonly reddish-brown in color, provincial for its cunning.

怀沙

Thinking of Sand

九章

滔滔孟夏兮,
草木莽莽。

O the summer stream does rush;
Plants and grass grow so lush.

伤怀永哀兮,
汨徂南土。

O the great woe I can't stand,
Rushing to Southern Land.

---

*Sand: name of a place that is today's Long Sand (Changsha), capital of Hunan Province. Young Sky (Shaohao) and God of Farming (Shennong) both founded their capitals at Sand, and now Long Sand, Changsha if transliterated, is its remaining site. And Sand or Long Sand as a fief was allotted by King Complete of Zhou to Spinning Bear (Yi Xiong), the first Viscount of Chu.

眴兮杳杳，

孔静幽默。

O It's dark all around,
Without a single sound.

郁结纡轸兮，

离愍而长鞠。

O pent-up gloom, endless pain;
In distress, distressed I remain.

抚情效志兮，

冤屈而自抑。

O while my will I express,
My chagrin and rue I down press.

刓方以为圜兮，

常度未替。

O a square can be a circle made!
No rule's been e'er mislaid!

易初本迪兮，

君子所鄙。

O your goal made otherwise,
Worthies will you despise.

九章

章画志墨兮，
前图未改。

O regulations arranged,
The plan cannot be changed.

内厚质正兮，
大人所盛。

O what's been nobly raised
Is what's by worthies praised.

巧倕不斲兮，
孰察其拨正。

O if Craftsman does not chop,
Who could know his art top?

玄文处幽兮，
蒙瞍谓之不章。

O a picture in dim light,
Blindman says, "It's not bright."

---

*Craftsman: name of a deft craftsman in Lord Mound's era.
*Blindman: name of a certain blind man bearing this name.

离娄微睇兮,

瞽以为无明。

Brighteye's eyes closed a bit,
Blindman says, "Dimly lit."

变白以为黑兮,

倒上以为下。

O what is white is called black;
What is front is called back.

凤皇在筊兮,

鸡鹜翔舞。

O a phoenix in a cage;
Ducks and hens on the stage.

---

*Brighteye: name of a man having very good sight in Lord Yellow's era. He is said to be capable of seeing an autumn weasel hair a hundred steps away.

*phoenix: a mythological bird of great beauty, said to be the only of its kind, which is supposed to live five or six hundred years before consuming itself by fire, rising again from its ashes to live through another cycle, a symbol of immortality. According to Chinese mythology, the phoenix only perches on phoenix trees, i.e. firmiana, only eats firmiana fruit, and only drinks sweet spring water, and this mythic bird appears only in times of peace and sagacious rule.

168

九章

同糅玉石兮,
一概而相量。

O rock and jade if you grate,
They will have the same weight.

夫惟党人鄙固兮,
羌不知余之所臧。

O if the partisans are rude and crude,
They'll never ever know my heart is good.

任重载盛兮,
陷滞而不济。

O to achieve, I aim higher;
But I am embogged in the mire.

怀瑾握瑜兮,
穷不知所示。

O in hand held is jade true;
To whom shall I its gleam show, who?

邑犬群吠兮,

吠所怪也。

O in the village dogs bark,
As they're stirred in the dark.

非俊疑杰兮,

固庸态也。

O who slander worthies true?
All those vulgarians do.

文质疏内兮,

众不知余之异采。

O I'm so simple and square,
But none of the crowd knows my brilliant flair.

材朴委积兮,

莫知余之所有。

O heaped is many a pole,
But nobody of them knows my role.

---

*dog: a domesticated carnivorous mammal (*Canis familiaris*), a subspecies of the gray wolf and is related to foxes and jackals. The dog, one of the two most ubiquitous and most popular domestic animals in the world, is of worldwide distribution and many varieties, noted for its adaptability and its devotion to man. The dog was domesticated in China at least 8,000 years ago and used as a hunter, as a poem in *the Book of Songs* says, "The dog bells clink and clink; / The hunter's handsome, a real pink."

九章

重仁袭义兮，

谨厚以为丰。

O I'd be a righteous man,
So that be reassured I can.

重华不可遻兮，

孰知余之从容！

O Hibiscus one can no more see;
Who knows I'm so natural and free?

古固有不并兮，

岂知其何故？

O all sages were not known of yore;
But whoever knows the wherefore?

---

*Hibiscus: Lord Hibiscus (cir. 2,277 B.C.-2,178 B.C.), Shun if transliterated, the Double-pupiled One, an ancient sovereign, a descendant of Lord Yellow (2,717 B.C.-2,599 B.C.), Lord Mound's son-in-law, regarded as one of Five Lords in prehistoric China.

汤禹久远兮,

邈而不可慕。

O Hotspring and Worm loom far;
How can we reach them up to par?

惩连改忿兮,

抑心而自强。

O swallow the pain and wrong;
I shall be strengthened, be so strong.

离愍而不迁兮,

愿志之有像。

O I don't repent, bearing the bane;
A good model I will remain.

进路北次兮,

日昧昧其将暮。

O for the night north I run,
As it's late, and setting is the sun.

---

*Hotspring: Hotspring of Shang (cir. 1,670 B.C.-1,587 B.C.), the founding king of Shang, who annihilated Xia with the help of two talents Captain and Chunghui as his two prime ministers.

*Worm: the founding lord of Xia, who took over the leadership from Hibiscus for his great success in controlling floods. Entrusted by Hibiscus to rid the kingdom of the deluge, Worm excavated mountains and hills and dredged rivers and streams all over the land like a god.

舒忧娱哀兮,
限之以大故。

九章

O forget worries there are,
As the end of life is not far.

乱曰:

The finale says,

浩浩沅湘,
分流汩兮。

The Yuan and Xiang far spread,
They rush, o rush ahead.

修路幽蔽,
道远忽兮。

The road rolls on to bend;
O where'er is its end?

怀质抱情,
独无匹兮。

My great faith one can see;
O no one is with me.

伯乐既没，

骥焉程兮。

On earth no more is Glee;
O connoiseur, where's he?

民生禀命，

各有所错兮。

The folk, the world, all those.
O God's the right to dispose.

定心广志，

余何畏惧兮？

Rest reassured instead!
O there is nothing to dread.

曾伤爰哀，

永叹喟兮。

I can't stop griefs, a try;
O I heave a long sigh.

---

*Glee: Glee One, a horse connoisseur called Shine Sun (Yang Sun), a subject of Lord Solemn of Qin (?-621 B.C.), reputed to be well versed in discerning the choice equestrian blood among horses, now often used as a metaphor for a person who discovers, recommends, raises and uses talents, a good judge of talent.

世溷浊莫吾知,
人心不可谓兮。

The world's turbid and none does know me;
O people's heart one can never see.

知死不可让,
愿勿爱兮。

I know my death I can't avoid;
O leave me alone, not coyed.

明告君子,
吾将以为类兮。

Those who have a broad mind,
O let me tell you, I'll join your kind.

九章

绘画：沈子琪

思美人

The Beauty I Miss

九章

思美人兮，
擥涕而竚眙。

O the beauty I miss;
Tears swept away, I gaze like this.

媒绝而路阻兮，
言不可结而诒。

O the road is blocked, no go-between;
Though sincere, I can't say what I mean.

蹇蹇之烦冤兮，
陷滞而不发。

O faithful but wronged, I've to bear the woe;
In dilemma, I cannot go.

申旦以舒中情兮,

志沈菀而莫达。

O each day I wish my wish were expressed,
But I cannot, feeling so depressed.

愿寄言于浮云兮,

遇丰隆而不将;

O I would ask a cloud to send my news;
Stopped by Rich Plump, it can but refuse.

因归鸟而致辞兮,

羌迅高而难当。

O I would ask a goose to send my word;
But I can't find one, high-flown the bird.

---

*Rich Plump: God of Rain or God of Clouds.
*goose: wild goose, an undomesticated goose that is caring and responsible, taken as a symbol of benevolence, righteousness, good manner, wisdom, and faith in Chinese culture.

九章

高辛之灵盛兮，
遭玄鸟而致诒。

O High Sen had virtue great and rare;
A black-bird for him did gifts prepare.

欲变节以从俗兮，
媿易初而屈志。

O I would change to follow the vain dust;
Ashamed, I should keep my will, I must.

独历年而离愍兮，
羌冯心犹未化。

O for years I have suffered countless pains;
As e'er, my embitterment remains.

---

*High Sen: referring to Lord Call (Diku), Lord Yellow's great-grandson, born at High Sen, that is, today's High Sen (Gaoxin), Shang Knoll (Shangqiu), Henan Province.
*black-bird: a legendary bird in Chinese mythology, mentioned in *Seas and Mountains*, a Chinese geographic book of myths and marvels.

宁隐闵而寿考兮，

何变易之可为！

O I'd rather bear the sorrow till old;
How can I let go of what I hold?

知前辙之不遂兮，

未改此度。

O I know the way ahead won't be smooth;
I won't betray the truth.

车既覆而马颠兮，

蹇独怀此异路。

O the cart is capsized, and the horse tired;
I'll go on the unique road desired.

勒骐骥而更驾兮，

造父为我操之。

O the steeds are harnessed for the new cart;
Lord Go holds the rein, playing his part.

---

*Lord Go: Chaofu if transliterated, a good groom and driver in the Zhou dynasty, who escorted King Solemn of Zhou to his visit of Mother West at Mt. Queen.

迁逡次而勿驱兮,

聊假日以须时。

九章

O slow down and linger, no strides, no haste,
Just to while time away, a good taste.

指嶓冢之西隈兮,

与曛黄以为期。

O I point to the west side of Mt. Tomb;
Twilight is the bedtime for the groom.

开春发岁兮,

白日出之悠悠。

O spring comes, the sun does shine;
The sun moves good hours forward, so fine.

---

*Mt. Tomb: a mountain in today's Gansu Province.

吾将荡志而愉乐兮,

遵江夏以娱忧。

O I abandon myself to the great glee,
As the Long and Summer flow, so free.

擥大薄之芳茝兮,

搴长洲之宿莽。

O in vast grass, angelica I amass,
And in Long Shoal I pick lodging-grass.

惜吾不及古人兮,

吾谁与玩此芳草?

O I can't see ancient men far away;
With whom to play with the grass in our play?

---

*the Long and Summer: the Long River and the Summer River that flows into the Long River.
*angelica: an aromatic herb, used as a decoration for a sash or pendant in ancient times.
*Long Shoal: a legendary place in Chinese mythology, probably a shoal in the Long River or the Summer River in this poem.

解萹薄与杂菜兮，

备以为交佩。

九章

O lord, you pick pig sprouts and weeds aground
To make sashes, to the waist bound.

佩缤纷以缭转兮，

遂萎绝而离异。

O rings and loops are so loved by my lord,
Fragrant grass is left to die, ignored.

吾且儃佪以娱忧兮，

观南人之变态。

O I pace and linger to allay my woe;
Those sycophants tiptoe to and fro.

---

*pig sprout: *Polygonum aviculare*, an annual herbaceous plant often found on roadside or waterside, used as medicine and food, especially food for pigs, in ancient China, also known as armstrong.

窃快在中心兮,

扬厥冯而不竢。

O I will seek inner glee and pride
And cast all my resentment aside.

芳与泽其杂糅兮,

羌芳华自中出。

O the fragrance of flowers blends with filth cursed;
From within elegant blossoms burst.

纷郁郁其远承兮,

满内而外扬。

O the elegance disseminates wide,
As brims inside and spreads outside.

情与质信可保兮,

羌居蔽而闻章。

O love and faith I can still well maintain;
My fame spreads afar from this domain.

令薜荔以为理兮,

惮举趾而缘木。

O climbing fig, be my go-between made,
But to climb the tree I feel afraid.

绘画：沈子琪

因芙蓉而为媒兮,

惮褰裳而濡足。

九章

O hibiscus, be my match-maker made,
But to cross the stream I feel afraid.

登高吾不说兮,

入下吾不能。

O climbing tree, I'm not very pleased;
Crossing the stream, I'm not so eased.

固朕形之不服兮,

然容与而狐疑。

O to such a thing I'm not very used;
I cannot go ahead, so confused.

---

*hibiscus: any of various malvaceous herbs, shrubs and trees of the genus *Hibiscus*, having numerous species in the mallow family (*Malvaceae*) that are native to warm temperate and tropical regions, blowing large, showy flowers of various colors.

广遂前画兮,

未改此度也。

O to finish what I've planned,
I've never ever changed my stand.

命则处幽吾将罢兮,

愿及白日之未暮也。

O I'm destined to live in the dark, so tired;
Before night falls I would finish what I've desired.

独茕茕而南行兮,

思彭咸之故也。

O alone, alone, southbound I go on,
And I do miss what Cord Peng had done.

*Cord Peng: a patriotic minister under King Chow in the Shang dynasty, who drowned himself after his failure in his remonstrance to his king. Yuan Qu followed his example when exiled.

惜往日

Missing the Bygone Day

九章

惜往日之曾信兮,
受命诏以昭时。

O woe, I was once trusted by my lord
To draft edicts for the state restored.

奉先功以照下兮,
明法度之嫌疑。

O the deeds of former kings could glare,
And the flawed rules we tried to repair.

国富强而法立兮,
属贞臣而日娭。

O with laws we made our state a great power;
Lord and subjects could have their free hour.

秘密事之载心兮,
虽过失犹弗治。

O we put in heart secrets of the state;
My errors our lord would tolerate.

心纯庞而不泄兮,

遭谗人而嫉之。

O so honest, nothing I would disclose;
I was slandered by flunkies, all those!

君含怒而待臣兮,

不清澄其然否。

O our lord was angered with me, so stern;
No wrong or right would he e'er discern!

蔽晦君之聪明兮,

虚惑误又以欺。

O the courtiers did hoodwink our lord's eyes,
And cheated him with rumors and lies.

弗参验以考实兮,

远迁臣而弗思。

O without proof you believed the whole lot,
Hence abandoning me without thought.

信谗谀之溷浊兮,

盛气志而过之。

O their balderdash you did choose to trust,
In ire censuring me as unjust.

九章

何贞臣之无罪兮,
被离谤而见尤。

O your faithful subject is not to blame;
Why do they bite and my worth defame?

惭光景之诚信兮,
身幽隐而备之。

O so wronged, I'm ashamed to face the sun;
To the dark recesses I would run!

临沅湘之玄渊兮,
遂自忍而沉流。

O on the bank of the river so deep,
Choking down my anger, I would leap.

卒没身而绝名兮,
惜壅君之不昭。

O at last I would die, no name, no more,
Our lord's fatuousness I deplore.

君无度而弗察兮，
使芳草为薮幽。

O our lord, excessive, can nothing see,
In wild woods the fragrant grass will be.

焉舒情而抽信兮，
恬死亡而不聊。

O where shall I my loyalty explain?
I'd rather die than useless remain.

独障壅而弊隐兮，
使贞臣为无由。

O I'm blocked alone in the wild, wild sand,
So I can no longer serve my land.

闻百里之为虏兮，
伊尹烹于庖厨。

O I hear Miles was once in servitude,
And Captain once a cook cooking food.

---

*Miles: Slave Miles (cir. 725 B.C.-621 B.C.), a great politician and thinker of the State of Qin, who helped to make Qin a powerful state in Lord Solemn's reign. He was sent as a slave, a part of Lady Solemn's dowry, to Qin and then fled to Chu. Lord Solemn bought him for five sheepskins from a market and appointed him as a minister.

*Captain: Captain (1,649 B.C.-1,550 B.C.), Yin Yi if transliterated, a statesman, thinker, founding commander of Shang and one of the founders of Wordism. Captain worked as Hotspring's counselor and prime minister.

吕望屠于朝歌兮，

宁戚歌而饭牛。

九章

O Great Grand was once a butcher in Morn,
And Halberd fed cows, knocking at horn.

---

*Great Grand: an influential strategist and statesman. Though he was a butcher at his young age, Great Grand remained diligent in hardship, expecting to display his ability for the country one day, but he did not make any achievement before he was 70 years old. He went west at the age of 72, fishing as he was waiting for King Civil of Zhou, and finally won his appreciation.
*Morn: referring to Mornsong, Zhaoge if transliterated, the capital of Shang, in today's Qi County, Henan Province, founded by King Wuding (1250 B.C.-1,192 B.C.), the twenty-third king of Shang.
*Halberd: Halberd Peace, a meritorious statesman of Qi in the Spring and Autumn period. In his early age, Peace was poor and had no access to officialdom. When Lord Column of Qi passed by, Peace knocked on an ox horn and sang out his frustration and attracted the lord's attention.

不逢汤武与桓缪兮，

世孰云而知之。

O if no Spring, Martial, Column, Solemn there,
Who in the world could e'er know their flair?

吴信谗而弗味兮，

子胥死而后忧。

O Wu's king did not repent when they lied;
Clerk Wu was exhumed after he died.

---

*Spring: referring to Hotspring of Shang (cir. 1,670 B.C.-1,587 B.C.), the founding king of Shang, the fourteenth generation grandson of Lord Call's son, Deeds, who was allotted the fief of Shang by Lord Mound for his great merits in assisting Worm to draw off the deluge.
*Martial: referring to King Martial (?-1,043 B.C.), the founding king of Zhou, who reigned only three years before his death from illness.
*Column: referring to Lord Column of Qi (?-643 B.C.), the sixteenth monarch of the State of Qi, the leader of the Five Hegemons in the Autumn and Spring Period.
*Solemn: referring to Marquis Solemn of Qin (682 B.C.-621 B.C.), the ninth monarch of Qin, one of the Five Hegemons in the Autumn and Spring Period.
*Wu: the State of Wu (12 Century B.C.-473 B.C.), a vassal state in the lower reaches of the Long River, i.e., the Yangtze River, annexed by the State of Yue.
*Clerk Wu: Clerk Wu (559 B.C.-484 B.C.), a minister and militarist of the State of Wu during the late years of the Spring and Autumn Period. At his old age, Clerk's suggestion was denied and he was alienated by the king. The king of Wu, irritated by Clerk's complaints, gave the latter a sword to commit suicide. After his death, the king put his body in a leather bag and threw it into a river.

九章

介子忠而立枯兮，
文君寤而追求。

O Mail, a just soul, died hugging a tree;
Lord Civil did search where he might be.

封介山而为之禁兮，
报大德之优游。

O the mountain was named Mail, all kept away,
The lord for his grace would him repay.

---

*Mail: Mail (?-636 B.C.), Zhitui of Jie if transliterated, remembered for his loyalty and integrity. In the Spring and Autumn period, Double Ear, a prince of Jin, escaped from the disaster in his state with his follower, that is Mail (zhitui). In great deprivation, Double Ear almost starved to death, and Mail fed him with flesh cut off his thigh. When Double Ear was crowned Lord Civil of Jin, Mail retreated to Mt. Silk Floss with his mother when feeling neglected. To drive him out, Lord Civil set the mountain on fire, but Mail did not give in and was burned with his mother, hugging a tree.
*Lord Civil: Lord Civil of Jin (697 B.C.-628 B.C.), named Double Ear, the twenty-second lord of the State of Jin, the second of the Five Hegemons.

思久故之亲身兮,

因缟素而哭之。

O thinking of his old comrade beside,
In mourning apparel loud he cried.

或忠信而死节兮,

或訑谩而不疑。

O someone would for his faithfulness die;
Someone would swindle and play so high.

弗省察而按实兮,

听谗人之虚辞。

O without proving what is false or true,
You would trust those who do nonsense spew.

芳与泽其杂糅兮,

孰申旦而别之?

O fragrance and luster can blend so well;
Who can the difference so clearly tell.

何芳草之早殀兮,

微霜降而下戒。

O why does fragrant grass die, in wind tossed?
Because they take no guard against frost.

九章

谅聪不明而蔽壅兮,
使谗谀而日得。

O our lord has been so hoodwinked indeed;
A good life the slanderer could lead.

自前世之嫉贤兮,
谓蕙若其不可佩。

O villains are always jealous, alas;
Why all say one can't wear fragrant grass?

妒佳冶之芬芳兮,
嫫母姣而自好。

O jealous of one's charming graceful way,
Mom would her coquettish airs display.

---

*Mom: Momu if transliterated, remembered as an ugly woman, Lord Yellow's fourth wife or concubine. She helped Lord Yellow defeat Lord Fire and Great Bug (Chiyou) and invented the mirror, originally a piece of honed stone.

虽有西施之美容兮，
谗妒入以自代。

O tho someone may have West Maid's charming face,
Gossips, rumors would replace her grace.

愿陈情以白行兮，
得罪过之不意。

O my true feelings I would now explain,
But I have come to suffer the pain.

情冤见之日明兮，
如列宿之错置。

O my love and wrongs one is sure to find,
Just like the stars in the sky aligned.

*West Maid: one of the most famous ladies in Chinese history, once a laundry maid in the State of Yue (2032 B.C.-222 B.C.), which was then a tributary to the State of Wu. Because of her beauty, West Maid was selected to be trained in Yue's palace, and sent to the King of Wu as a spy. She quickly won the king's affection, making him indulged in her charm. As a result, the State of Wu waned and perished.

九章

乘骐骥而驰骋兮,

无辔衔而自载;

O I'd ride my horse and gallop amain,
But I have no harness, bits or rein.

乘氾泭以下流兮,

无舟楫而自备。

O I'd get on the raft and downstream flow,
But I have no oar wherewith to row.

背法度而心治兮,

辟与此其无异。

O you do not rule with law but your mind,
As clear as similes you may find.

---

*horse: a large herbivorous solid-hoofed quadruped (*Equus caballus*) with coarse mane and tail, of various strains: Ferghana, Mongolian, Kazaks, Hequ, Karasahr and so on and of various colors: black, white, yellow, brown, dappled and so on, domesticated about four thousand years go, reared as a pet, employed as a beast of draught and burden and especially for riding upon. Horses have played an important part in Chinese history and human civilization, widely employed in agriculture, transportation and warfare.

宁溘死而流亡兮,

恐祸殃之有再。

O I would die, by water washed away,
For fear disasters come on one day.

不毕辞而赴渊兮,

惜壅君之不识。

O I'd leap and jump into the abyss;
A pity, our lord does not know this.

橘颂

Ode to the Orange

九章

后皇嘉树,

橘徕服兮。

受命不迁,

生南国兮。

King of trees, of the best,
O accustomed, you're grand.
Now settled, never moved,
O you grow in South Land.

---

*orange: *Citrus reticulata Blanco*, a reddish, yellow, round, edible citrus fruit, with a sweet, juicy pulp; any of various evergreen trees (genus *Citrus*) of the rue family bearing this fruit.

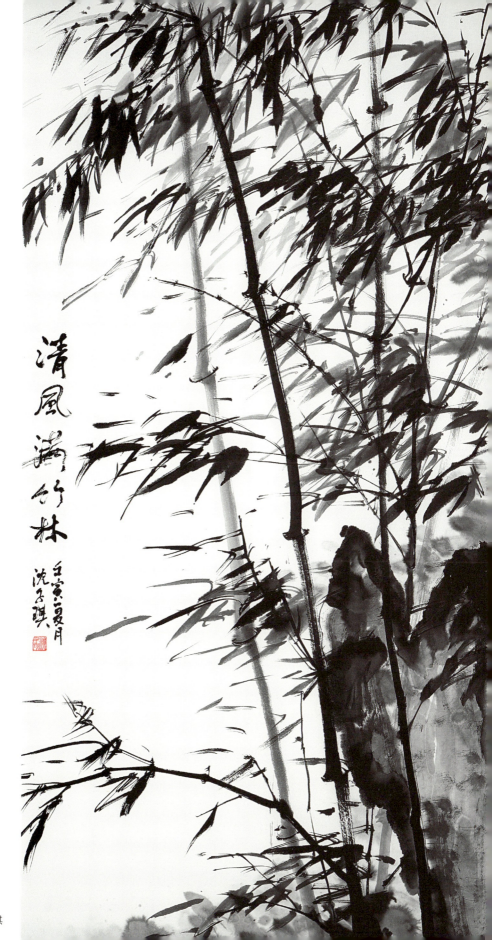

绘画：沈子琪

深固难徙,
更壹志兮。
绿叶素荣,
纷其可喜兮。

九章

Deeply rooted, so staid,
O you're focused and willed.
With leaves green and flowers white,
O with such glee you're fulfilled.

曾枝剡棘,
圆果抟兮。
青黄杂糅,
文章烂兮。

Leaf upon leaf, with thorns,
O you've fruit round and fine.
With yellow out of green,
O you have hues to shine.

精色内白，

类任道兮。

纷缊宜修，

姱而不丑兮。

With pure skin, a white heart,
O you embrace the Way.
So fragrant and so spruce,
O not plain, grace you display.

嗟尔幼志，

有以异兮。

独立不迁，

岂不可喜兮。

How great, a great young will!
O unique you're to me!
Independent, unchanged,
O isn't your state our glee?

*the Way: the Kingly Way, the righteous tradition initiated by Lord Mound and Lord Hibiscus in ancient Chinese government or the Way of Heaven, the natural or divine ultimate force in the cosmos.

九章

深固难徙,
廓其无求兮。
苏世独立,
横而不流兮。

So settled, moved no more,
O broad-minded, you stand tall.
Straightforward and detached,
O to the dust you don't fall.

闭心自慎,
终不失过兮。
秉德无私,
参天地兮。

Circumspect and discreet,
O you've never gone awry.
Unselfish and virtuous,
You tower twixt earth and sky.

愿岁并谢,

与长友兮。

淑离不淫,

梗其有理兮。

With you I would share all,
O be good friends for long.
Graceful and not obscene,
O you're rational and strong.

年岁虽少,

可师长兮。

行比伯夷,

置以为像兮。

Although you are so young,
You're my teacher, my bro.
You are well placed in here,
O my icon like Great Bow.

*Great Bow: Bow One, so named because of being firstborn. There are two notables known by the name Great Bow or Bow One in Chinese history. The first one is the grand priest in Lord Mound's time, in charge of rites and criminal law; the second is the elder prince of the lord of Lonebamboo, a vassal state of Shang, who died of starvation at Mt. Firstshine to maintain his rectitude.

悲回风

Mourning the Whirling Wind

九章

悲回风之摇蕙兮,

心冤结而内伤。

O the whirling wind sways the basil grass;
Melancholy, all worries, alas.

物有微而陨性兮,

声有隐而先倡。

O so weak, it's easy to be hurt now;
The wind is forceful, unseen its sough.

---

*basil: a popular, tender, annual aromatic herb of the *Lamiaceae* family (or *Labiatae* family), is native to India and some other Asian countries, widely used in cooking.

夫何彭咸之造思兮,

暨志介而不忘!

O why then does Cord Peng attract our call?
His will we cannot forget at all!

万变其情岂可盖兮,

孰虚伪之可长?

O how can all those changes cover the fact?
How can vanity long long protract?

鸟兽鸣以号群兮,

草苴比而不芳。

O birds and beasts each to the other cry;
Fresh grass will lose its scent near grass dry.

鱼葺鳞以自别兮,

蛟龙隐其文章。

O fish display their unique shining scales;
Krakens sink to hide their beauteous tails.

---

*Cord Peng: a patriot in the Shang dynasty, who drowned himself after his failure in his remonstration of King Chow, a notorious hair-raising tyrant. Yuan Qu, our poet, followed him as an example and drowned himself in the River Miluo.
*kraken: a legendary sea monster of northern seas, looking like something between a dragon and a giant octopus.

九章

故荼荠不同亩兮,

兰茝幽而独芳。

O maror 'n beet ne'er grow in the same field;
Orchids in the recesses scent yield.

惟佳人之永都兮,

更统世以自贶。

O only beauties can maintain their grace;
Through the ages they can still be ace.

眇远志之所及兮,

怜浮云之相羊。

O my will would go far, so far away,
But cloud-like, in the sky it does stay.

---

*maror: *Sonchus oleraceus*, a kind of edible bitter herb, naturalized in all countries neighboring China and is anthropogenically distributed almost worldwide. The entire plants are used medicinally.

*beet: a kind of edible sweet herb, a plant with a thick root, often fed to animals or used to make sugar.

介眇志之所惑兮,

窃赋诗之所明。

O no one can understand my great will,
So I can but make a verse to trill.

惟佳人之独怀兮,

折若椒以自处。

O with my melancholy, I here stand,
With pollia and pepper sprays in hand.

曾歔欷之嗟嗟兮,

独隐伏而思虑。

O I release sighs again and again;
In this wildness I can't cease my pain.

涕泣交而凄凄兮,

思不眠以至曙。

O my tears flow and flow in my dire plight;
I toss and I turn throughout the night.

---

*pollia: a perennial herb with horizontal long rhizomes and erect or ascending stems and blowing actinomorphic flowers.
*pepper: referring to pepper from the ancient State of Shen, also known as Qin pepper or Chinese pepper, usually used as a spice, a symbol of fecundity in Chinese culture.

210

九章

终长夜之曼曼兮,

掩此哀而不去。

O the long long night now comes to an end;
As e'er, my sorriness does extend.

寤从容以周流兮,

聊逍遥以自恃。

O I will wander and roam everywhere;
Free and unfettered, I'll kill my care.

伤太息之愍怜兮,

气于邑而不可止。

O woe, my wretchedness I do deplore;
I cannot stop my overwhelming sore.

纠思心以为纕兮,

编愁苦以为膺。

O with all my worries a sash I sew
And I weave an underwear with rue.

折若木以弊光兮，

随飘风之所仍。

O I break off a spray from a Lithe Tree,
To shut out sunlight and wind from me.

存彷佛而不见兮，

心踊跃其若汤。

O all haze before me, I can see not;
My heart boils and churns like water hot.

抚珮衽以案志兮，

超惘惘而遂行。

O I wake up and straighten out my gown;
I go out, stupefied and pressed down.

岁曶曶其若颓兮，

时亦冉冉而将至。

O how time flows, so fast it does elapse;
My life will be o'er, and I will collapse.

---

*Lithe Tree: a giant mulberry-like fairy tree, ten thousand kilometers east of China, against which the sun rises, also known as Fuguesome.

绘画：沈子琪

菸蘅槁而节离兮,

芳以歇而不比。

九章

O scirpus 'n asarum dry, their leaves lop;
Fragrance no more, all comes to a stop.

怜思心之不可惩兮,

证此言之不可聊。

O my sorrow goes on and tends to prevail,
And my confession comes to no avail.

宁溘死而流亡兮,

不忍此心之常愁。

O I would rather die or drift for e'er;
I couldn't tolerate this constant care.

---

*scirpus: *Scirpus triangulatus*, a large genus of widely distributed annual or perennial sedges (family *Cyperaceae*) that bear solitary or much-clustered spikelets containing perfect flowers with a perianth of bristles.
*asarum: commonly known as wild ginger, whose beauty lies in its small, jug-shaped flowers and heart-shaped leaves, which in some species are dark green, shiny and mottled with cream.

孤子吟而抆泪兮,

放子出而不还。

O orphan-like, I wipe my tears, alack,
A deserted son that can't go back.

孰能思而不隐兮,

照彭咸之所闻。

O who can e'er think of this without pain?
I'll follow Cord Peng, along his lane.

登石峦以远望兮,

路眇眇之默默。

O I climb up the hill and afar peer;
The road is so silent, like death sheer.

入景响之无应兮,

闻省想而不可得。

O I've come to a world, no sound, no brink;
I cannot even see, or hear, or think.

愁郁郁之无快兮,

居戚戚而不可解。

O no pleasure, all depression, all try;
The skein of sorrow I cannot untie.

心鞿羁而不开兮,

气缭转而自缔。

九章

O my heart is bound, no release, no hope,
Tightened, tightened with many a rope.

穆眇眇之无垠兮,

莽芒芒之无仪。

O all dead silence, no bottom, no bound;
The wilderness spreads, no form, no sound.

声有隐而相感兮,

物有纯而不可为。

O the fall whisper's weak, but all can feel;
The orchid's pure but can't to all appeal.

藐蔓蔓之不可量兮,

缥绵绵之不可纡。

O the world affairs one can ne'er e'er control;
Adrift, adrift, there loafs my saddened soul.

愁悄悄之常悲兮，
翩冥冥之不可娱。

O the lasting grief does choke me, so sad;
I dance in darkness, not relieved, not glad.

凌大波而流风兮，
讬彭咸之所居。

O I move, I move, following the tide,
To the place where Cord Peng did abide.

上高岩之峭岸兮，
处雌蜺之标颠。

O I climb up the cliff, clouds to command,
And on top of the rainbow I stand.

据青冥而攄虹兮，
遂儵忽而扪天。

O I breathe down to the rainbow on high,
And all of a sudd'n, I stroke the sky.

吸湛露之浮源兮，
漱凝霜之雰雰。

O I suck up dewdrops shining so bright;
And I gargle with snowflakes so white.

九章

依风穴以自息兮,
忽倾寤以婵媛。

O against the wind cave, I myself rest,
Then I wake up, with sadness obsessed.

冯昆仑以澂雾兮,
隐㟽山以清江。

O against Mt. Queen, I see all haze spread;
By Rush I see rivers rush ahead.

惮涌湍之磕磕兮,
听波声之汹汹。

O the rapids strike the sheer cliff to shake;
The waves rolling down do my ears quake.

---

*Mt. Queen: Mt. Kunlun if transliterated, the most sacred mountain in China. It starts from the eastern Pamir Plateau, stretches across New Land (Xinjiang) and Tibet, and extends to Blue Sea (Qinghai), with an average altitude of 5,500-6,000 meters. In Chinese myths, Mt. Queen is where Mother West dwells.

纷容容之无经兮,

罔芒芒之无纪。

O the river tumbles and tumbles on;
In endless whiteness, the waters run.

轧洋洋之无从兮,

驰委移之焉止?

O the combers rush and o'er there extend;
Bends, curves, where will they come to an end?

漂翻翻其上下兮,

翼遥遥其左右。

O the billows roar up and down with might;
Then they rumble, grumble, left and right.

氾滥滥其前后兮,

伴张驰之信期。

O the breakers surge up and then abate;
Tides and ebbs happen at a fixed date.

---

*Rush: Mt. Rush, Mt. Min if transliterated, a mountain range stretching from Kansu to Northwest Sichuan.

观炎气之相仍兮,

窥烟液之所积。

九章

O I watch summer heat rise and remain
And vapor congeal as mist and rain.

悲霜雪之俱下兮,

听潮水之相击。

O sad, frost and snow fall down to the ground;
Tidewater strikes, a deafening sound.

借光景以往来兮,

施黄棘之枉策。

O shine and shade go out and come again;
I make a whip with a crooked cane.

求介子之所存兮，
见伯夷之放迹。

O I search for Mail's place where to abide,
And find Mt. Fisrtshine, Bow's mountainside.

心调度而弗去兮，
刻著志之无适。

O I think aloud: With them I will stay,
Nowhere will I go, o nay, o nay.

曰

The finale:

吾怨往昔之所冀兮，
悼来者之愁愁。

O of my insensible quest I complain,
And deplore my fright, my endless pain.

*Mt. Firstshine. located in today's Weiyuan County. It is the highest of all mountains there, so it is the first to receive sunshine, hence the name, and it is famous because two princes from the State of Lonebamboo called Bow One and Straight Three died of starvation here for their rectitude.
*Bow: referring to Bow One or Great Bow, the grand priest in Lord Mound's time, in charge of rites and criminal law.

九章

浮江淮而入海兮，
从子胥而自适。

O I'll follow the river to the seas;
Side by side with Clerk, I'll myself please.

望大河之洲渚兮，
悲申徒之抗迹。

O in the great river there looms a shoal;
Sad, I think of Plume, a noble soul.

骤谏君而不听兮，
重任石之何益？

O lord, you don't listen, I'm left alone;
What's the use of sinking with a stone?

---

*Clerk: Clerk Wu (559 B.C.-484 B.C.), Grand Tutor of the Crown Prince of Chu, then a minister and militarist in the State of Wu during the late years of the Spring and Autumn Period.
*Plume: Plume Shentu: a loyal minister in the last years of Shang, who drowned himself carrying a boulder after his failure to persuade King Chow.

心絓结而不解兮,

思蹇产而不释。

O my heart is wound and wound like a knot;
With hundreds of lasting cares I'm fraught.

天问

Asking the Sky

天问

曰：遂古之初，
谁传道之？

I'd ask: As Beginning began
Who passed it, by which man?

上下未形，
何由考之？

Not formed, Heaven and earth;
Who's it that gave them birth?

冥昭瞢闇，
谁能极之？

Chaos, so blurred and dim,
Who can reach to the brim?

---

*Beginning: the primal state when the universe was created out of nothing.

冯翼惟象，

何以识之？

This icon does there rise;
This who can recognize?

明明闇闇，

惟时何为？

Shine o shine, shade o shade,
When was it like this made?

阴阳三合，

何本何化？

Shine and Shade and Man too,
What's the root, fruit, or cue?

圜则九重，

孰营度之？

The dome has nine folds, true!
Who has measured it, who?

惟兹何功，

孰初作之？

What a project, how grand!
Who built it as well planned?

斡维焉系，

天极焉加？

The axis of earth, oh, where?
Where's the pole? You know e'er?

八柱何当，

东南何亏？

Where do Eight Pillars face,
Southeast a sunken place?

九天之际，

安放安属？

Within the nine broad skies,
Where are their links and ties?

天问

---

*Eight Pillars: the eight pillars propping up the sky in Chinese mythology, also a metaphor for the mainstay of a cause, enterprise or project.

隅隈多有,

谁知其数?

Corners, edges, all those,
Who knows the count, who knows?

天何所沓?

十二焉分?

Where do Sky and Earth meet?
Why twelve parts so discreet?

日月安属?

列星安陈?

How suns and moons align?
How are stars placed to shine?

出自汤谷,

次于蒙汜。

Suns rise from Sunrise Dell
And in Haze Flow they dwell.

---

*Sunrise Dell: the place where the ten suns rise according to Chinese mythology.
*Haze Flow: the place where the ten suns set for the night according to Chinese mythology.

自明及晦，
所行几里？

From dawn to eve, they run;
How far there for day one?

夜光何德，
死则又育？

Why with her wax and wane,
The moon, dead, lives again?

厥利维何，
而顾菟在腹？

What benefit is there
Now her abdomen holds a hare?

女岐无合，
夫焉取九子？

Miss Offset's no man fine;
Where has she gotten children nine?

天问

---

*Miss Offset: a beautiful erotic goddess who has nine sons without having had sex according to Xia's folklore.

伯强何处?

惠气安在?

Where is our God, First Force?
Where does His spirit course?

何阖而晦?

何开而明?

Why dark when it's closed tight?
Why, when oped, is it bright?

角宿未旦,

曜灵安藏?

Before Spica wakes wide;
Where does the sunlight hide?

不任汩鸿,

师何以尚之?

Water o'erfloods the brim;
Why did all those recommend him?

---

*First Force: equivalent to Aeolus in the west, sometimes understood as God of Pestilence.
*Spica: a spectroscopic binary star, Alpha in the constellation Virgo.

金曰:"何忧,

何不课而行之?"

天问

All said, "nothing to dread,
Why not let him go and do instead?"

鸱龟曳衔,

鲧何听焉?

Like turtles, suns proceed;
Why didn't Great Fish heed?

顺欲成功,

帝何刑焉?

He would succeed, as found;
Why punished by Lord Mound?

---

*turtle: referring to Beshee, a tortoise-like beast in mythology. In China, tablets of great importance were usually carried on the back of a turtle-like creature called Beshee, which is said to be a figure of the sixth son of the dragon, who is strong and keen on carrying a heavy load.
*Great Fish: Count of Tower (an area in the vicinity of Mt. Tower), father of Great Worm, the First King of Xia (21 B.C.-16 B.C.), a forerunner of water conservation in Chinese culture.
*Lord Mound: Mound (2,377 B.C.-2,259 B.C.), Yao if transliterated, Lord Yellow's descendant, the saintly leader of Allied Nations (or Clans) before the founding of Xia (cir. 2070 B.C.-1600 B.C.). Divine and noble, Mound has been regarded as one of Five Lords in ancient China.

永遏在羽山，

夫何三年不施？

He's been shut at Mt. Plume for long;
It's three years; why not free him, what's wrong?

伯禹愎鲧，

夫何以变化？

From Great Fish comes Worm now;
Can him manage the flood, how?

纂就前绪，

遂成考功。

He'll finish what's not done;
The great war must be won!

何续初继业，

而厥谋不同？

To succeed his sire, the poor man,
Can he contrive a different plan?

*Worm: the founding lord of Xia, who took over the leadership from Lord Hibiscus. It was said that Lord Mound was put in jail, having lost his morality, and Lord Hibiscus died in a moor when he was in a tour. The poet borrowed the ancient legend to imply that the reign of King Bosom of Chu was in danger of being destroyed.

天问

洪泉极深,

何以窴之?

How profound the abyss!
Who could fill it, fill this?

地方九则,

何以坟之?

The good earth has parts nine;
How can we it define?

河海应龙?

何尽何历?

How does Duct Dragon draw
So rivers and seas pour?

---

*Duct Dragon: Flying Dragon or Winged Dragon, which helped Great Worm in controlling flood. It drew on the ground with its tail and thereby Worm dug rivers so that the flood was conducted to the sea.

鲧何所营？

禹何所成？

What has Great Fish ill done?
What has Lord Worm well won?

康回冯怒，

墬何故以东南倾？

Co-Work's angered, so hot;
Why does Southeast collapse, collapse a lot?

九州安错？

川谷何洿？

How are Nine Realms disposed?
For dredging what's proposed?

东流不溢，

孰知其故？

The river eastwards ill flows?
What's the reason? Who knows?

---

*Co-Work: God of Water, who controls flood in Chinese mythology, noted for his skillfulness. In history, Co-Work was Lord Flame's great-great-grandson, a sovereign and a chieftain of a clan.
*Nine Realms: the nine areas of Chinese, or referring to China itself. China, the Middle Kingdom, was divided into nine realms as early as Lord Yellow's era. After the deluge during Mound's reign, Worm delineated them once more.

白日生之悠悠 沈子琪写於

绘画:沈子琪

东西南北，

其修孰多？

North and south, east and west,
Which's the most, which's the best?

南北顺椭，

其衍几何？

North-south a narrow thong,
How long is it, how long?

昆仑悬圃，

其尻安在？

Mt. Queen, an Eden sheer;
Where is its end, its rear?

---

*Mt. Queen: Mt. Kunlun if transliterated, one of the most sacred mountains in China. It starts from the eastern Pamir Plateau, stretches across New Land (Xinjiang) and Tibet, and extends to Blue Sea (Qinghai), with an average altitude of 5,500-6,000 meters. In Chinese mythology, Mt. Queen is where Mother West dwells.

增城九重,

其高几里?

Step-up Town is nine-layer;
Where is its top, o where?

四方之门,

其谁从焉?

Mt. Queen has gate towers four;
Who are those who there pour?

西北辟启,

何气通焉?

There ope west gate, north gate;
What airs there circulate?

日安不到?

烛龙何照?

Where sunlight reaches not,
What can Lighter do, what?

---

*Step-up Town: a legendary place on Mt. Queen.
*Lighter: a dragon having fire or candle in its mouth, one eye representing the sun and the other the moon.

羲和之未扬，
若华何光？

She-Her's not here to drive;
From where does light arrive?

何所冬暖？
何所夏寒？

Where's the winter warm still?
Where's the summer so chill?

焉有石林？
何兽能言？

Where does stone make a wood?
What beasts can speak, so good?

---

*She-Her: the mother of the sun or the dyad of Goddess of Sun and Goddess of Calendar in Chinese mythology.
As is said, She-Her, as Goddess of Sun, drives the sun across the sky.

焉有虬龙，

负熊以游？

Which dragonet's much vim?
Which bear can better swim?

雄虺九首，

儵忽焉在？

The serpent has heads nine;
Where's it, show me a sign?

何所不死？

长人何守？

Where does one never die?
On what does he rely?

*dragonet: a fabulous dragon-like animal with or without horns, smaller than a common dragon.
*bear: any of a family (*Ursidae*) of large, heavy omnivorous carnivores that walk flat on their soles of their feet and have shaggy fur and a very short tail: bears are native to temperate and arctic zones.
*serpent: a snake, especially a large or poisonous one. It's usually used as a metaphor for a sneaking, treacherous person, as is exemplified in *Genesis* of *the Bible*.

靡萍九衢,

枲华安居?

Where are duckweed's roots twined?
Where can you male hemp find?

灵蛇吞象,

厥大何如?

Can snakes elephants eat?
How big are they? How great?

---

*duckweed: any of several small, disk-shaped, floating aquatic plants common in streams and ponds.
*male hemp: a species of hemp that blows flowers but does not bear fruit.
*snake: an ophidian reptile, having a greatly elongated, scaly body, no limbs, and a specialized swallowing apparatus, a symbol of indifference, malevolence, cattiness, and craftiness in Chinese culture.
*elephant: a massively built, almost hairless ungulate mammal of Asia and Africa, the largest of existing land animals, having a flexible proboscis or trunk, and the upper incisors developed as tusks valued as the chief source of ivory.

黑水玄趾，

三危安在？

The Dark Stream sees black toes;
Where are Three Risks, o those?

延年不死，

寿何所止？

If one can death suspend,
When will a long life end?

鲮鱼何所？

鬿堆焉处？

Where is a wizard dace?
Where is a ghost bird's place?

*the Dark Stream: name of a river.
*Three Risks: Mt. Three Risks, the first attraction in today's Dunhuang, Gansu Province.
*wizard dace: a legendary fish like ace which is any of a number of small, slim, active freshwater fishes of the carp family, *Cyprinidae*.

244

羿焉彈日？

乌焉解羽？

天问

King Archer shoots nine suns?
The sun spot falls at once?

禹之力献功，

降省下土四方。

Now having finished a deed grand,
Worm descends to inspect all the land.

---

*King Archer: a legendary figure in Chinese mythology. In Mound's age, there were ten suns in the sky, making it hard for anything to survive. To save the people, King Archer shot down nine of them. And he wiped out six demonic pests, conquered River God and saved Miss Sedate, that is, Goddess of the Luo.

焉得彼嵞山女，
而通之於台桑？

Where does he the Mt. Mud fairy find?
At Mulberry with her he is twined.

闵妃匹合，
厥身是继。

He marries her at once
To bear daughters and sons.

胡维嗜不同味，
而快鼌饱？

Why do they have the same taste to share
To have their love affair?

*Mt. Mud: in today's Cao County, Shandong Province, where Lord Worm married a young woman and summoned all vassals of the land after his success in conquering the flood.
*the Mt. Mud fairy: referring to the young woman Lord Worm met and married at Mt. Mud.
*Mulberry: Mulberry Mound, also known as Mt. Scene in the east of today's Cao County, Shandong Province.

绘画：沈子琪

248

启代益作后，

卒然离蠥。

Then Ope does king become;
To banes he does succumb.

何启惟忧，

而能拘是达？

Why does Ope suffer pain
And, confined, can be free again?

皆归射鞠，

而无害厥躬。

It's owing to his deed
That from disasters he's been freed.

---

*Ope: Qi if transliterated, King Ope, Worm's son and successor, the second king of Xia, reigning from 1978 B.C. to 1963 B.C. He was crowned king after Brim One (Poyi), also known as Shade Great (?-1973 B.C.), famous for having helped Lord Worm in conquering the great flood, an inventor of the well in Chinese culture.

何后益作革,

而禹播降?

Why does Brim's bliss end soon?
Why does Worm have long boon?

启棘宾商,

《九辩》《九歌》。

In Heaven, Ope, a guest,
Is with *Counts* and *Songs* blessed.

何勤子屠母,

而死分竟地?

Does the son have his mother killed?
With her bones all the ground is filled.

---

*Brim: Brim One (cir. 21 Century B.C.), Boyi if transliterated, also called Shade One, the first son of Moor Potter (cir. 2,219 B.C.-2,113 B.C.). Brim helped Lord Worm in controlling the great deluge and was given the family name Ying by Hibiscus and was then made an administrator in King Worm's reign and a prime minster in King Ope's reign, second only to King Ope in power. He was the forefather of the clans or states of Fei, Xu, Zhao, Qin, Liang, Jiang, Huang and so on.

Counts and *Songs*: referring to *Nine Counts* and *Nine Songs*, cantatas with verse recitatives composed during Lord Worm's reign, the former of which is a dance cantata about the delineation of the nine parts of the land and the latter about the benefits of the nine achievements—the six resources of water, fire, metal, wood, clay and grain and the three principles of justice, utility and well-being.

帝降夷羿,

革孽夏民。

Mound sends King Archer here
To free the folks of fear.

胡射夫河伯,

而妻彼雒嫔?

Why do you shoot River God there
And capture Luo's Maid, his wife fair?

冯珧利决,

封豨是射。

With your thumb ring and bow,
The boar's shot at one go.

---

*River God: God of the Yellow River, the spirit of Fastbow (Fengyi) who got drowned in the river, as is said.
*Luo's Maid: also known as Miss Sedate, King Archer's sister, who was drowned in the Luo River and became its spirit and was therefore called Goddess of the Luo.
*boar: also called wild boar or wild pig, a mature uncastrated male of the wild members of the pig species *Sus scrofa*, family *Suidae*. It is bristly haired, grizzled, and blackish or brown in color and stands up to 90 cm (35 inches) tall at the shoulder.

何献蒸肉之膏，

而后帝不若？

Why do you offer meat so well greased
While God of Heaven is not pleased?

浞娶纯狐，

眩妻爰谋。

 Soak Cold will Pure Fox wed,
So they cut Archer's head.

何羿之射革，

而交吞揆之？

Archer could pierce a hide;
Could they finish the parricide?

阻穷西征，

岩何越焉？

So blocked is their way west;
Can they pass the hill's crest?

---

*God of Heaven: God for short, the one Supreme Being, self-existent and eternal, the infinite creator, sustainer, and ruler of the universe, regarded as omniscient, omnipresent and omnipotent.
*Soak Cold: Soak (cir. 2013 B. C.-1933 B.C.), surnamed Cold, a usurper of the Xia throne.
*Pure Fox: King Archer's wife, also Known as E'erfair (Chang-e) in Chinese mythology.

化而为黄熊,

巫何活焉?

Great Fish has become a brown bear;
Can the witch change it e'er?

咸播秬黍,

莆雚是营。

Sedge 'n silvergrass has grown,
Where black millet was sown.

何由并投,

而鲧疾修盈?

Why is he chased and maimed?
Is Great Fish so wicked, ill-famed?

---

*sedge: a grasslike cyperaceous herb with flowers densely clustered in spikes: widely distributed in marshy places.
*silvergrass: genus *Miscanthus*, of about 10 species of tall perennial grasses in the family *Poaceae*, native primarily to southeastern Asia.
*black millet: *Panicum miliaceum*, also known as proso millet, native to Asia and naturalized, now widespread over much of the rest of the world. Proso millet is grown for its grain, a staple food in many parts of Asia and Africa, having been cultivated in China since prehistoric times.

白蜺婴茀,

胡为此堂?

If with white plumes one's clad,
Can he make a good fad?

安得夫良药,

不能固臧?

Where can we good elixir gain
And can it long retain?

天式从横,

阳离爰死。

Crisscross is our great Way;
One dies as Shine's away.

大鸟何鸣,

夫焉丧厥体?

How Great Bird does now cry!
Why all too soon does it there die?

---

*Way: the Heavenly Way or kingly Way, the ultimate natural and governmental law based on the Word.
*Shine: positive or active vim or air of life in contrast with Shade, the opposite.
*Great Bird: the incarnation of Prince of Front of Zhou (567 B.C.-549 B.C.), the first son of King Spirit of Zhou (795 B.C.-771 B.C.). Prince of Front died young, and after his death he rose to the sky, riding a white crane, and became immortal.

天问

萍号起雨,
何以兴之?

Lord Cloud cries for a rain;
Raise a storm would he fain?

撰体协胁,
鹿何膺之?

Its physique soft and meek
Can Deer everywhere seek.

鳌戴山抃,
何以安之?

A turtle bears the hill;
How can it stay put, still?

---

*Lord Cloud: name of Master of Rain.
*Deer: Flydeer, Flying Deer, God of Wind, which is said to have a bird's head and a deer's body.

释舟陵行，

何之迁之？

The boat is stopped and moored?
How can Giant Human ford?

惟浇在户，

何求于嫂？

When Pour Cold is indoors,
Will he trap his in-laws?

何少康逐犬，

而颠陨厥首？

Why can Young Prime lead out his hound
And cut Pour's head to fall aground?

女歧缝裳，

而馆同爱止。

Miss Offset does clothes mend
And with Pour Cold does her time spend.

---

*Giant Human: a giant in the Land of Great Dragons, mentioned in *Sir Line*.
*Pour Cold: Soak Cold's son, a strong man.
*Young Prime: Shaokang if transliterated, the sixth king of the Xia dynasty, the inventor of Chinese wine.
*Miss Offset: Pour Cold's sister-in-law.

何颠易厥首,
而亲以逢殆?

天问

Why does Young Prime Pour Cold's head claim?
Struggling, he is killed all the same.

汤谋易旅,
何以厚之?

When Hotspring drills his men,
How does he treat them then?

覆舟斟寻,
何道取之?

His ship he does capsize;
What's that where he relies?

---

*Hotspring: Hotspring of Shang (cir. 1,670 B.C.-1,587 B.C.), Tang if transliterated, the founding king of Shang, who annihilated Xia with the help of two talents Captain and Zhonghui as his two prime ministers.

桀伐蒙山,

何所得焉?

Stump does launch a campaign;
At Haze what will he gain?

妹嬉何肆,

汤何殛焉?

How Happy goes at will!
How does Hotspring Stump kill?

舜闵在家,

父何以鳏?

At home Hibiscus stays;
Why unwed, as Dad weighs?

*Stump: Fowl Stump (?-1,600 B.C.), Jie if transliterated, a tyrant and the last lord of the Xia dynasty.
*Haze: Mt. Haze, name of a vassal state.
*Happy: Meixi if transliterated, King Stump's first concubine, his favorite, who later exterminated Xia in cooperation with Captain, the first prime minister of Shang.
*Hibiscus: Lord Hibiscus, Shun if transliterated, the Double-pupiled Man, an ancient sovereign, a descendant of Lord Yellow, regarded as one of Five Lords in prehistoric China.

绘画：沈子琪

尧不姚告，

二女何亲？

If Mound says no instead,
How can his two girls wed?

厥萌在初，

何所亿焉？

If at the start no sprout,
Who can bring the fruit out?

璜台十成，

谁所极焉？

Chow's mound is ten tiers high;
Who can this feat come by?

登立为帝，

孰道尚之？

By Heaven he's made lord;
For what is he adored?

---

*Mound: Lord Mound (2,377 B.C.-2,259 B.C.), Yao if transliterated, regarded as Lord Call's son. Divine and noble, he initiated the system of demising the throne, and has been regarded as one of Five Lords in ancient China.

天问

女娲有体,
孰制匠之?

Newwha's body like this,
Whose making? Hers or his?

舜服厥弟,
终然为害。

Loving his brother much,
Hibiscus is hurt as such.

---

*Newwha: Nüwa if transliterated, the Creator of animals and humans in Chinese mythology. In the beginning Newwha created fowls, dogs, pigs, sheep, oxen and horses respectively in the first six days and created mankind on the seventh day. According to other sources, she was Hidden Spirit's younger sister, who devised wind instruments and set down the rites of marriage, affirming that men and women with the same surname should not unite in wedlock.
*his brother: referring to Hibiscus's brother named Elephant.

何肆犬豕，

而厥身不危败？

Pig or dog, he does bump;
Why does he not fail or fall or slump?

吴获迄古，

南岳是止。

The State of Wu stays long;
For Mt. South where all throng.

孰期去斯，

得两男子？

Who knows the reason then?
It's because of two men.

---

*pig: any swine, especially the unweaned young of the thick-bodied domesticated species.
*dog: a domesticated carnivorous mammal (*Canis familiaris*), of worldwide distribution and many varieties, noted for its adaptability and its devotion to man, its master.
*the State of Wu: a southern vassal state of Zhou, founded by Usetwo, King Civil of Zhou's uncle in the 12th century B.C., the early years of Zhou, and subjugated and annexed by the State of Yue in 437 B.C.
*Mt. South: referring to Mt. Whir first mentioned in China's earliest geography book *Seas and Mountains*, probably a mountain in today's Linfen, Shanxi Province.
*two men: referring to Greatone and Usetwo, two sons of Father Verity of Zhou. They moved to the east, today's Jiangsu Province, to leave the throne to Throughfour, his younger brother, who can be remembered as King Civil of Zhou's father.

缘鹄饰玉,

后帝是飨。

Bronze tripods for a treat,
Whereby our king can eat.

何承谋夏桀,

终以灭丧?

By use of Captain's plan,
Killed is Stump, the bad man.

帝乃降观,

下逢伊挚。

Hotspring goes all around
And there Captain is found.

天问

何条放致罚,

而黎服大说?

At Twigsough Stump will punished be;
Why do the folk jump high with glee?

简狄在台,

喾何宜?

Jane Plume at Jade Mound, eased,
Why is Call pleased?

玄鸟致贻,

女何喜?

Black Bird sends bride price here;
Why does she cheer?

---

*Twigsough: Mingtiao if transliterated, at Twigsough Mound, an ancient battleground where Hotspring defeated Stump, hence exterminating the first recorded Kingdom of Xia, in today's Anyi County, Shanxi Province.
*Jane Plume: a beauty from the State of Song (Yousong), Lord Call's second concubine, who gave birth to Deeds, the forefather of Shang.
*Call: Lord Call, Diku if transliterated, one of the Five Sovereigns in prehistoric China, Lord Plump Head's nephew, Lord Yellow's great-grandson.
*Black Bird: name of a swallow-like legendary bird, traditionally explained as the Ebon Bird or the Mystic Bird, similar to the phoenix in ancient China.

该秉季德,

厥父是臧。

Inheriting Sprout's grace,
Swine's won his father's praise.

胡终弊于有扈,

牧夫牛羊?

Why is he at last in Hu Land slain,
Shepherding in this plain?

干协时舞,

何以怀之?

When Swine gets up to dance,
Why will she him romance?

---

*Sprout: Swine's father, also known as Marquess Murk.
*Swine: Marquess Swine or Swine Wang (1854 B.C.-1803 B.C.), a descendant six generations from Deeds, who was a forefather of Shang.
*Hu Land: the State of Hu, which is Hu County in today's Sha'anxi Province.

平胁曼肤，

何以肥之？

This girl has creamy skin;
Why can Swine her love win?

有扈牧竖，

云何而逢？

The shepherd in Hu Land,
Why can he have her hand?

击床先出，

其命何从？

He flees, hard struck his bed;
How can he keep his head?

恒秉季德，

焉得夫朴牛？

Inheriting Sprout's grace,
Where has Ever got the cow ace?

何往营班禄，

不但还来？

Why does he give out rank and pay?
Can he come his safe way?

*Ever: Sprout's son, Swine's younger brother.

昏微循迹,

有狄不宁。

天问

When Dark follows the track,
Plume Land will fall, alack.

何繁鸟萃棘,

负子肆情?

Why do they flock on jujube trees?
Will they their chicks' wives please?

眩弟并淫,

危害厥兄。

The younger's a loose life,
Lusting for his bro's wife.

---

*Dark: Dim-Dark, Hunwei if transliterated, nephew of Swine Wang (1854 B.C.-1803 B.C.), a forefather of Shang (1600 B.C.-cir. 1046 B.C.), the second dynasty in Chinese history.
*Plume Land: a northern area inhabited by barbarians called Plumes or Di if transliterated.
*jujube: *Ziziphus jujuba* Mill., any of a genus of trees or shrubs of the buckthorn family, especially the common thorny jujube, the lotus tree.

何变化以作诈,

而后嗣逢长?

Why does he, so crafty, always scheme,
But his descendants richly teem?

成汤东巡,

有莘爰极。

Hotspring does east campaign
And reaches Shen's domain.

何乞彼小臣,

而吉妃是得?

Why can he get a servant fine
And also a good concubine?

水滨之木,

得彼小子。

By the riverside tree,
He's got the servant wee.

---

*Shen: name of an ancient state, one of the three Shens: West Shen, South Shen and East Shen.

夫何恶之，
媵有莘之妇？

Why then despised is he
And is sent away as dowry?

汤出重泉，
夫何辠尤？

Spring sees Hotspring shut in;
What's his crime, what's his sin?

不胜心伐帝，
夫谁使挑之？

He'll beat Stump for a shameful sore;
Who's stirred up this terrible war?

会朝争盟，
何践吾期？

The vassals will unite;
Will they faithfully fight?

---

*Spring: referring to Double Spring, where Hotspring, the first king of Shang, was jailed.

苍鸟群飞,

孰使萃之?

In a flock the hawks fly;
Who's gathered them, o why?

列击纣躬,

叔旦不嘉。

They vow: Chow killed must be;
But Dawn does not agree.

---

*hawk: a diurnal bird of prey, a type of large birds that catch small birds and animals for food, a metaphor for one who takes a militant or combative attitude (as in a dispute) and advocates immediate vigorous action.

*Dawn: given name of Prince of Zhou, the 4th son of King Civil, a younger brother of King Martial, the greatest statesman of all time. After King Martial died, the king was too young to reign, so Prince of Zhou became a regent. During his regency, he put forward fundamental laws and regulations in various aspects, and improved the patriarchal rite-music system, the feudal system, and the well-farmland system. The political, economic and cultural measures of early Zhou were mainly his exploits.

何亲揆发足,

周之命以咨嗟?

天问

Why make the plan for Vance now, why?
Zhou founded, we've just relieved a sigh.

授殷天下,

其位安施?

Shang's kingdom's divine too,
Where to place Chow the true?

---

*Vance: given name of King Martial of Zhou (?-1,043 B.C.), the founder and pioneering king of Zhou, the second son of Boom, who was officially entitled Count West, posthumously entitled King Civil (1,152 B.C.-1,056 B.C.). He inherited the throne when Boom, i.e. King Civil died in 1,056 B.C.
*Shang: the Shang dynasty (1600 B.C.-1046 B.C.), the second of the recorded dynasties of China. In 1600 B.C., Hotspring and his troops defeated Xia at Twigsough (Mingtiao) and was elected at a summit of three thousand lords of vassal states as the sovereign of Shang. He founded his capital at Bo.

反成乃亡，

其罪伊何？

Transgression means a bane;
What's his fault, to be slain?

争遣伐器，

何以行之？

With arms the states will rise;
How can Vance mobilize?

并驱击翼，

何以将之？

The troops advance as planned;
How will Vance them command?

昭后成游，

南土爰底。

King Glare tours in a cart
And stops in the south part.

*King Glare: King Glare of Zhou (?-977 B.C.), son of King Health of Zhou, the fourth king of Zhou. After his succession, he continued to prosper Zhou and expanded its territory.

厥利惟何,

逢彼白雉?

What does he achieve there?

Just seen a pheasant fair?

穆王巧梅,

夫何为周流?

Solemn his horse astride,

Why does he travel the world wide?

---

*pheasant: a long-tailed gallinaceous bird noted for the gorgeous plumage of the male, often regarded as wild chicken in Chinese culture.
*Solemn: King Solemn of Zhou (cir. 1026 B.C.- cir. 922 B.C.), King Glare's son, the fifth king of Zhou, one of the most capable and legendary kings in Chinese history. He employed Marquess Lü as Minister of Justice, who wrote *Book of Penalties* and expanded Zhou's territory in all directions, capturing five kings of Dog Batons in the west and conquering Xu in the east and summoning all vassals at Mt. Mud to pacify the southeast borders.
*horse: a hoofed herbivorous mammal of the family *Equidae*, comprising a single species, *Equus caballus*, divided into numerous varieties.

绘画：沈子琪

环理天下，

夫何索求？

He goes and looks around;
For where will he be bound?

妖夫曳炫，

何号于市？

The wizard shouts o'er there,
Why shouting in the fair?

周幽谁诛？

焉得夫褒姒？

Who has King Dark there slain?
Where did he P'aossu, the belle, gain?

天问

---

*King Dark: King Dark of Zhou (?-771 B.C.), the twelfth king of Zhou, remembered as a despotic and debauched tyrant who splashed muddy water on the cinders of Zhou's past glory.
*Baosi: a beauty captured from the State of Bao, the second queen of King Dark of Zhou. She, as is often believed, caused Zhou to collapse, hence the end of Western Zhou.

天命反侧,

何罚何佑?

Heaven plays fast and loose;
Fined are these, blessed are those?

齐桓九会,

卒然身杀。

Lord Column Nine allies;
He is trapped and there dies.

彼王纣之躬,

孰使乱惑?

That King Chow, that poor cad,
Who's made this tyrant mad?

---

*Lord Column: Lord Column of Qi (?-643 B.C.), the sixteenth monarch of the State of Qi, who developed Qi into a powerful state through political and military reforms and became the leader of the allies called Five Hegemons in the Autumn and Spring Period.
*Nine: referring to the nine vassal states led by Lord Column.
*King Chow: King Sen (1105 B.C.-1046 B.C.), or King Sin, the last king of Shang, who had executed severe laws and waged large-scale wars in the northwest and southeast, which triggered conflicts among reigning groups and weakened the foundation of Shang's reign. In folk's version, King Chow was usually described as a violent tyrant indulging in luxury and desires.

何恶辅弼，

谗谄是服？

Why detest aides so good;
Why trust slanderers rude?

比干何逆，

而抑沈之？

What is wrong with Bican?
Why do they stop this man?

雷开阿顺，

而赐封之？

Storm Switch, a man of cant,
Why has he got a grant?

---

*Bican: Bican (1110 B.C.-1047 B.C.), Bigan if transliterated, the prime minister of Shang, King Chow's uncle. Having served the court as an imperial tutor since he was 20, he was loyal and caring for the people. He often remonstrated King Chow with blunt words. Bican's admonition finally irritated King Chow and he was martyred, his heart taken out.

*Storm Switch: a crafty minister under King Chow of Shang, as is said.

何圣人之一德,

卒其异方?

Why do all the saints have the same grace
But do in different ways?

梅伯受醢,

箕子详狂?

Plum First meat paste is made;
Dustpan's a mad man played.

稷维元子,

帝何竺之?

King Corn, First Son adored,
Why by Lord Call abhorred?

---

*Plum First: a vassal lord under Shang, also known as Marquis E. He was parched after his remonstrance with King Chow against his lasciviousness and cruelty.
*Dustpan: Dustpan (?-1082 B.C.), Ji if transliterated, King Chow's uncle, a grand teacher, who fled Shang to Korea and founded his kingly kingdom in the east after his failure to persuade King Chow into mending his ways, esteemed as one of the Three Worthies at the end of the Shang dynasty.
*King Corn: Houji if transliterated, born at Mt. Corn, Lord Yellow's great-great-grandson, Lord Call's first son, Zhou's forefather, esteemed as God of Farming.
*Lord Call: Diku if transliterated, Lord Yellow's great-grandson, one of the Five Sovereigns in prehistoric China.

278

投之于冰上，

鸟何燠之？

He is thrown away onto ice;
Birds warm him with wings nice.

何冯弓挟矢，

殊能将之？

Why does one carry a bow?
Why does one all crops sow?

既惊帝切激，

何逢长之？

With his birth God is gratified;
Why does his offspring tide?

天问

伯昌号衰,

秉鞭作牧。

For decadence Boom's cried;
He'd over Yong preside.

何令彻彼岐社,

命有殷国?

Why does King Martial chair Zhou's shrine
And rules Shang, as divine?

迁藏就岐,

何能依?

At Offset he's his day;
Would the folks obey?

---

*Boom: given name of King Civil of Zhou, the spiritual founder of Zhou. Boom inherited from his father Throughfour the title of Count West, a vassal lord of Yong or Yongzhou, under the suzerainty of Shang.
*Yong: one of the ancient nine realms, Boom's fief under Shang before the founding of the Zhou dynasty.
*King Martial: King Martial (?-1,043 B.C.), the founder of Zhou, the second son of Boom (1,152 B.C.-1,056 B.C.), who was posthumously titled King Civil. King Martial inherited the throne when Boom died in 1,050 B.C. and adopted the system of enfeoffment based on five ranks: duke, marquess, count, viscount, and baron.
*Mt. Offset: a mountain south of today's Phoenix Flying County.

殷有惑妇,

何所讥?

天问

Chow by Daji seduced,
What satire used?

受赐兹醢,

西伯上告。

With his son, the paste, by,
Boom cries out to the sky.

---

*Daji: an imperial concubine of King Chow (1,075 B.C.-1,046 B.C.), the last emperor of Shang. It is said that King Chow spent too much time with Daji and neglected government affairs, and as a result, Shang was overthrown by Zhou.
*paste: Count West's eldest son, Fief Old One (Boyikao), was made into meat paste by King Chow, who gave it to Count West (posthumously recognized as King Civil of Zhou) as food to test the latter's sainthood.

何亲就上帝罚,

殷之命以不救?

Why has Chow been punished for his sin?
Why can none save the Kingdom of Yin?

师望在肆,

昌何识?

Then Great Grand is in the fair;
Why met by Boom there?

鼓刀扬声,

后何喜?

Swords are swayed west and east;
Why is the king pleased?

---

*the Kingdom of Yin: alias of Shang. The Kingdom of Shang was first addressed Yin by Zhou folk who showed their contempt by referring it to Yin Plain, Shang kings' hunting ground.
*Great Grand: an influential strategist and statesman and one of the founders of Zhou. Though he was a butcher at his young age, Great Grand remained diligent in hardship, expecting to display his ability for the country one day, but he did not make any achievement before he was 70 years old. He went west at the age of 72, fishing as he waited for King Civil, and finally won his appreciation.

武发杀殷,

何所悒?

Now Vance has wiped out Yin,
Why does gloom swell in?

载尸集战,

何所急?

The corpse carried to fight,
Why are they in plight?

伯林雉经,

维其何故?

Chow hangs himself on fire;
What's there to inquire?

天问

---

*Yin: generally referring to Shang, and specifically the later part of the Shang dynasty, when Pangeng moved his capital from Chockful (Qufu) to Yin, which is today's Peaceshine (Anyang), Henan Province.

何感天抑墜,

夫谁畏惧?

Vance shakes Heaven and earth there laid;
Of whom is he afraid?

皇天集命,

惟何戒之?

When Yin was made divine,
Why no warning or fine?

受礼天下,

又使至代之?

Since Chow's been on the throne;
Why is he replaced, far away thrown?

初汤臣挚,

后兹承辅。

Captain, a servant mere,
Is later made premier.

何卒官汤,

尊食宗绪?

Why like Hotspring, divine,
Is he placed in the shrine?

绘画：沈子琪

勋阖梦生，

少离散亡。

Door, Dream's grandson high born,
When young, was apart torn.

何壮武厉，

能流厥严？

He looks so strong and bold;
His fame spreads far as told.

彭铿斟雉，

帝何飨？

Why can Peng's pheasant food
Please Lord Mound's mood?

---

*Door: referring to Doorshut (547 B.C.-496 B.C.), Helü if transliterated, King Doorshut of Wu, who was the first grandson of Life Dream, Dream for short.
*Dream: Life Dream (620 B.C.-561 B.C.), Shoumeng if transliterated, a capable monarch of Wu, who made Wu a prosperous vassal state and was addressed king ever since.
*Peng: Sire Peng (1237 or 1214 B.C.-1100 B.C.), Lord of Peng, enfeoffed with the State of Great Peng (What is today's Xuzhou) by Lord Mound. He is known as a Wordist and gastronome, said to have lived eight hundred years, having married 49 wives and born 54 sons.

受寿永多,
夫何久长?

Living long is a song;
Why can life be so long?

中央共牧,
后何怒?

The land ruled up and down,
Who's angered the crown?

蜂蛾微命,
力何固?

Moths have so short a life;
Why strong in their strife?

天问

惊女采薇，

鹿何祐？

Vetch picking shocks a maid;
Why have they the deer's aid?

北至回水，

萃何喜？

North in Backwaters there,
They're starved in blessed air?

兄有噬犬，

弟何欲？

Scene has a hound so brave;
His bro does it crave?

---

*vetch: any of a genus (*Vicia*) of herbaceous twining leguminous plants including some grown for fodder and green manure, a recurring image in classic Chinese literature.
*deer: a ruminant (family *Cervidae*), having deciduous antlers, usually in the male only, as the moose, elk, and reindeer. Deer are closely related to Chinese life. Deer hide is a precious gift, especially presented to a female and a deer is usually a symbol of imperial power as it is often a target of pursuit.
*Backwaters: referring to the Bent River under Mt. Firstshine, where the two princes from the State of Lonebamboo called Bowone (Boyi if transliterated) and Straightthree (Shuqi if transliterated) died of starvation for their rectitude.
*Scene: Lord Scene of Qin (?-537 B.C.), the nineteenth monarch of the State of Qin. In his reign for 39 years, he expanded Qin's territory to the midland of China.

天问

易之以百两,
卒无禄?

Can the dog two hundred carts cost?
The bro's his life lost.

薄暮雷电,
归何忧?

Thunder, lightning at eve,
What does them aggrieve?

厥严不奉,
帝何求?

No more state, no more task;
From God what to ask?

---

*God: also called God of Heaven, the infinite creator of everything out of nothing, which is the same with the Word in *the Bible*.

伏匿穴处，

爰何云？

In the cave hidden stay;
What have we to say?

荆勋作师，

夫何长？

They have died for the land;
How long can it stand?

悟过改更，

我又何言？

I've repented my way;
What more have I to say?

吴光争国，

久余是胜。

Wu has fought long with Chu;
We've long lost the war, phew!

---

*Chu: a vassal state of Zhou, a fief allotted to Spinning Bear (Yi Xiong), which became one of the powers in the Warring States period, its area including the regions of present-day Hunan and Hubei and neighboring areas as far as Sichuan, Henan, Shandong, Jiangsu and Zhejiang, conquered and annexed by Qin in 223 B.C.

何环穿自闾社丘陵,

爰出子文?

Why do they go around and cross the hill and glen
And give birth to Sir Wen?

吾告堵敖,

以不长。

I have said our lord, Tour,
Can survive no more.

---

*Sir Wen: the premier of Chu in King Complete of Chu's reign. He, a virtuous, capable and sagacious administrator, made great contributions to the consolidation and expansion of Chu.
*Tour: King Wall Tour of Chu (?-672 B.C.), name of a prince, King Civil of Chu's son, known as Tour of Chu, who was murdered by his brother five years after his succession.

何试上自予，

忠名弥彰？

Why has Complete murdered the lord
But got well-known, adored?

*Complete: referring to King Complete of Chu (?-626 B.C.), who usurped the throne from his elder brother Tour of Chu. With Sir Wen's help, King Complete formed an alliance with some states and conquered others such as Xuan, Huang, Ying, and Kui, thus expanded Chu territory.

招魂

Evocation

294

招魂

朕幼清以廉洁兮，
身服义而未沫。

O when young, my justice I tried to raise,
With righteousness never to abase.

主此盛德兮，
牵于俗而芜秽。

O I'm virtuous and humane;
But I've been defiled by the mundane.

上无所考此盛德兮，
长离殃而愁苦。

O the lord does not my great virtue extol;
Woe, woebegone, what a lonely soul!

帝告巫阳曰：

God of Heaven tells Witch Shine:

"有人在下，

我欲辅之。

魂魄离散，

汝筮予之。"

"A worthy's down below;
To help him I will go!"
His soul's out of the brim;
Please divine to save him."

*God of Heaven: God for short, the Supreme Being, Providence, who is understood as the self-existent, eternal and ultimate spirit, the infinite creator, sustainer, and ruler of the universe, regarded as supernatural, with transcendental properties: omniscient, omnipresent and omnipotent.
*Witch Shine: name of a sorceress and doctor in Chinese mythology, and name of a mountain as well.

招魂

巫阳对曰：

"掌梦！

上帝其难从；

若必筮予之，

恐后之谢，

不能复用。"

Witch Shine replies aside:
"Lord of Dream does preside!
Lord, I can't follow your command.
If I divine to give a hand,
He might vanish so soon,
No use for that back blown."

巫阳焉乃下招曰：

Therefore, Witch Shine alights to call:

---

*Lord of Dream: an official in ancient China, who's in charge of oneiromancy, that is, taking dreams as omens whereby to divine.

魂兮归来！

去君之恒干，

O do come back, soul!
Why have you left your body whole?

何为四方些？

舍君之乐处，

而离彼不祥些！

Why do you wander all around?
Why do you flee your bliss unbound?
You may be cursed, having left the ground.

魂兮归来！

东方不可以讬些。

O come back, soul, it's pressed;
East Land is not a place for you to rest.

长人千仞，

惟魂是索些。

A giant, like a long pole,
May be searching now for your soul.

绘画：沈子琪

十日代出，

流金铄石些。

Ten suns send light by turn;
All ore and stone melt while they burn.

彼皆习之，

魂往必释些。

They're used despite all curse;
But your soul is bound to disperse.

归来兮！

不可以讬些。

O come back, it's pressed;
O'er there, not at all can you rest.

魂兮归来！

南方不可以止些。

O do come back, soul!
South Land is not a place for you to stroll.

招魂

雕题黑齿,

得人肉以祀,

以其骨为醢些。

Black-toothed and tattoo-faced,
For rites they slaughter humans chased,
And make their flesh and bones into meat paste.

蝮蛇蓁蓁,

封狐千里些。

Vipers crawl here and there;
Foxes run about everywhere.

---

*viper: any of a wide-spread family of venomous snakes, usually used as a metaphor for the vile.
*fox: any of several burrowing carnivores of the dog family, especially those of the genus *Vulpes*, smaller than wolves, having a pointed, slightly upturned muzzle, erect ears, and a long, bushy tail, commonly reddish-brown in color, provincial for its cunning.

雄虺九首,

往来倏忽,

Male serpents have heads nine;
Anything they can twine.

吞人以益其心些。

They swallow people for their heart and breast.

归来兮!

不可久淫些。

O come back, it's pressed!
Not so long can you o'er there rest.

魂兮归来!

西方之害,

流沙千里些。

O do come back, soul!
Disasters in the west,
Quick sands for a thousand miles roll.

---

*serpent: a limbless scaly elongate reptile, a snake, especially a large or poisonous one. It's usually used as a metaphor for a sneaking, treacherous person, a noxious creature that creeps, hisses, or stings.

旋入雷渊,
靡散而不可止些。

招魂

They're blown to the abyss;
How can they stop the dispersal, like this?

幸而得脱,
其外旷宇些。

So lucky, one is out;
It is dead silence all about.

赤蚁若象,
玄蜂若壶些。

Red ants, elephant-size,
Black wasps, like gourds arise.

---

*ant: a small social hymenopterous insect (family *Formicidae*), an emmet. The communities of ants, well organized according to their duties, are made up of winged males, females winged till after pairing and wingless neuters or workers.
*wasp: any of numerous hymenopterous insects, chiefly of the superfamilies of *Sphecoidea* and *Vespoidea*, of which the workers and females are provided with effective stings, often live in organized colonies.
*gourd: any of a family (*Cucurbitaceae*, the gourd family) of chiefly herbaceous tendril-bearing vines including the cucumber, melon, squash, pumpkin, and so on.

五谷不生，

丛菅是食些。

No grains there can grow fine;
All the folk on themeda dine.

其土烂人，

求水无所得些。

All are scorched by the sun;
There's no water to drink, there is none.

彷徉无所倚，

广大无所极些。

Lonely, nowhere can one rely;
No end of the vast comes to the eye.

归来兮！

恐自遗贼些。

O do come back!
You may be abused there, alack.

---

*themeda: usually called villous themeda, an annual or perennial tussock grass, often coarse, with culms tufted and leaf sheaths keeled.

招魂

魂兮归来！
北方不可以止些。

Come back, soul, it's so pressed;
North Land is not a place for you to rest.

增冰峨峨，
飞雪千里些。

Ice does make many piles;
Flying snow does fly many miles.

归来兮！
不可以久些。

O come back, pressed;
For so long you cannot there rest.

魂兮归来！
君无上天些。

O do come back, soul,
You can't stay in the sky, all sole.

虎豹九关,

啄害下人些。

Tigers, leopards gates guard;
They eat earthlings, so harsh and hard.

一夫九首,

拔木九千些。

A monster has heads nine
Can uproot many a giant pine.

豺狼从目,

往来侁侁些。

Wolves, jackals have long eyes;
To rush ahead each of them vies.

---

*tiger: one of the big cats, a large carnivorous feline mammal of Asia, with vertical black wavy stripes on a tawny body and black bars or rings on the limbs and tail, praised as king of all animals.
*leopard: a ferocious carnivorous mammal of the cat family of Asia and Africa, of a pale fawn color, spotted with dark brown or black, praised as King of Forest, regarded as an auspicious animal in Chinese culture.
*pine: a cone-bearing evergreen tree having needle-shaped leaves growing in clusters, a symbol of rectitude, fortitude and longevity in Chinese culture.
*wolf: a large carnivorous mammal related to the dog, regarded as ravenous, cruel, or rapacious, a metaphor for an invader or lecher in Chinese culture.
*jackal: a dog-like carnivorous mammal, reddish-brown or gray, smaller than a wolf, with a long bushy tail, feeding on small animals and on carrion as well.

招魂

悬人以嬉,

投之深渊些。

They fling people with glee
To the abyss deep as can be.

致命于帝,

然后得瞑些。

Reporting to God high,
You will breathe your last, thus to die.

归来!

往恐危身些。

Come back, try!
It's dangerous e'en in the sky.

---

*God: the perfect and all-powerful spirit or being that is worshiped all over the world as the one who created and rules the universe, in Chinese setting often pursued as the natural generating Word or the Word personalized and consecrated as Old Father of Heaven.

魂兮归来!

君无下此幽都些。

O do come back, soul,
Lord, do not go down to Hades, all sole.

土伯九约,

其角鬐鬐些。

Lord Earth, writhed in bends nine,
Has horns that like all knives do shine.

敦脄血拇,

逐人駓駓些。

Thick fat back stained with blood,
He chases men like a spurt of flood.

参目虎首,

其身若牛些。

A three-eyed tiger head
A body like a cow well-bred.

---

*Hades: the abode of the dead, and a euphemism for hell. It is usually called Yellow Spring in Chinese culture, because deep down earth water is yellow, and Yellow Spring belongs in the Nine Hells and Nine Springs.
*Lord Earth: God of Earth, usually representing the earth or land in general.

招魂

此皆甘人,

归来!

恐自遗灾些。

These monsters devour men,
Do come back;
You may suffer their fierce attack.

魂兮归来!

入修门些。

O do come back, soul,
Ent'r the gate, by the pole.

工祝招君,

背行先些。

The witch does the lord lead;
Back in front, he does speed.

秦篝齐缕,

郑绵络些。

Qin's pannier, Qi's silk bright,
And Zheng's brocade so light.

招具该备,

永啸呼些。

All the tools laid about,
The witch does long long shout.

魂兮归来!

反故居些。

O do come back, soul!
Come home, no more out stroll.

---

*Qin: the Qin State or the State of Qin (905 B.C-206 B.C.), enfeoffed as a dependency of Zhou by King Piety of Zhou in 905 B.C. and promoted to be a vassal state by King Peace of Zhou in 770 B.C., and exterminating Zhou's suzerainty in 221 B.C..

*Qi: the State of Ch'i (1,000 B.C.-221 B.C.), a vassal state of Zhou, allotted by King Martial to Great Grand in the first place, which developed into a powerful state in the Spring and Autumn period as the leader of the Five Hegemons and in the Warring State period, as one of the Seven Powers.

*Zheng: the State of Zheng (806 B.C.-375 B.C.), a fief allotted to Friend (yu), a son of King Through (li) and a brother of King Clare (xuan) of Zhou in the vicinity of Zhou's capital, which developed into an important vassal state famous for its economy, legal system, democracy and culture of poetry and music.

310

招魂

天地四方，

多贼奸些。

Heaven and earth profound
Have robbers all around.

像设君室，

静闲安些。

Like your house planned so well,
A place quiet, quiet to dwell

高堂邃宇，

槛层轩些。

Deep rooms and a high hall;
Good rails and columns tall.

层台累榭，

临高山些。

Layered mound and tiered bowers;
Face a mount that high towers.

网户朱缀,

刻方连些。

Carved doors adorned with red,
Checkered from foot to head.

冬有突厦,

夏室寒些。

Winter halls warm like wool;
Summer rooms seem so cool.

川谷径复,

流潺湲些。

The dale road twists and bends;
Far, far, the pool extends.

光风转蕙,

汜崇兰些。

The basil a wind blows;
From within fragrance flows.

---

*basil: a herb with a sweet smell that is used to add flavour in cooking, native to India and some other Asian countries.

经堂入奥,
朱尘筵些。

招魂

Blown to the hall like that,
Red dust falls on the mat.

砥室翠翘,
挂曲琼些。

Smooth rooms, green plumes, good look;
High wall, bright hue, jade hook.

翡翠珠被,
烂齐光些。

 Adorned with pearls, quilt bright,
How soft, how soft the light!

蒻阿拂壁,
罗帱张些。

Rush mat hung on the wall;
Gauze tent set in the hall.

纂组绮缟,

结琦璜些。

Colored strings combined;
Brilliant jade there aligned.

室中之观,

多珍怪些。

The furnishings so dear,
Adorned with jewels so queer.

兰膏明烛,

华容备些。

Candles give off clean light;
The belles' faces beam bright.

二八侍宿,

射递代些。

Sixteen girls for the night,
Each on shift, each in sight.

绘画：沈子琪

九侯淑女,

多迅众些。

Belles from Marquess Ghost's state,
Make a big crowd so great.

盛鬋不同制,

实满宫些。

Each hair-do being a chic style,
Belles fill harems each while.

容态好比,

顺弥代些。

So fair from face to face,
What unparalleled grace!

弱颜固植,

謇其有意些。

Their body like a beam;
Their charm so alluring like cream.

---

*Marquess Ghost: Marquess of the State of Uglies, one of the three most important grandees under Shang, who was killed, minced and made into meat paste by King Chow because the lady the former presented as a gift would not please the king, i.e the tyrant.

招魂

姱容修态,
絚洞房些。

Each one a flowering bloom,
Moving from room to room.

蛾眉曼睩,
目腾光些。

Beneath the brows eyes bright
Send out shimmering light.

靡颜腻理,
遗视矊些。

Her skin's tender like cream;
Her glance does seem to gleam.

离榭修幕,
侍君之闲些。

A big tent by the bower;
They serve the king for his free hour.

翡帷翠帐,

饰高堂些。

The emerald tent tall;
The brightly furnished hall.

红壁沙版,

玄玉梁些。

Scarlet wall, red board laid,
The giant beam like black jade.

仰观刻桷,

画龙蛇些。

On the rafter you find
Snakes with dragons combined.

*snake: an ophidian reptile, having a greatly elongated, scaly body, no limbs, and a specialized swallowing apparatus, a symbol of indifference, malevolence, cattiness, and craftiness in Chinese culture.

*dragon: Though variously understood as a large reptile, a marine monster, a jackal and so on in Western culture, it has been esteemed as a fabulous serpent-like giant winged animal, a totem of the Chinese nation and a symbol of benevolence and sovereignty in Chinese culture.

坐堂伏槛,

临曲池些。

招魂

In the hall gainst the rail;
At the pond by the trail.

芙蓉始发,

杂芰荷些。

To flower lotus begin,
Trapa leaves dotted in.

---

*lotus: one of the various plants of the waterlily family, noted for their large floating round leaves and showy flowers blooming in white or pink, a symbol of purity and elegance in Chinese culture, unsoiled though out of soil, so clean with all leaves green.
*trapa: a floating water-plant with heart-shaped leaves and edible seeds of two, three or four prongs that are ripe in autumn, an ever-recurring image in Chinese literature, like the lotus.

紫茎屏风，

文缘波些。

Water shields show mauve stems;
The ripples stir their hems.

文异豹饰，

侍陂陁些。

In leopard hide with frills,
Guardsmen safeguard the hills.

轩辌既低，

步骑罗些。

Lo, the carts with crests grand,
Aligned, soldiers there stand.

---

*water shield: a purple-flowered waterlily (*Brasenia schreberi*), having floating elliptic or ovate leaves coated underneath with a jelly-like substance, cherished as a local delicacy in the lower reaches of the Long River.

招魂

兰薄户树,
琼木篱些。

The door that orchids sees;
The hedge made of green trees.

魂兮归来!
何远为些?

O do come back, soul!
Why do you afar stroll?

室家遂宗,
食多方些。

The whole family's here
Plentiful is our cheer.

---

*orchid: any of a widely distributed family of terrestrial or epiphytic monocotyledonous plants having thickened bulbous roots and often very showy distinctive flowers, one of the four most important floral images in Chinese literature, which are wintersweet, orchid, bamboo, and chrysanthemum.

稻粱穱麦，
挐黄粱些。

Rice, rye, barley and wheat,
Mixed with millet to eat.

大苦醎酸，
辛甘行些。

Bitter, sour, all replete,
And all those hot or sweet.

肥牛之腱，
臑若芳些。

Beef, the sinew, so fat,
And tender, cooked like that.

---

*rice: an annual cereal grass, widely cultivated on wet land in warm climate. Rice has been cultivated in China for 6,000 to 9,000 years, dating back to the Neolithic Age according to archaeological finds.
*rye: secale cereale, cereal grass (family *Poaceae*) and its edible grain.
*barley: a cereal grass with dense, bearded spikes of flowers, each made up of three single-seeded spikelets.
*wheat: a grain yielding an edible flour, the annual product of a cereal grass (genus *Triticum*), introduced to China from West Asia more than 4,000 years ago, used as a staple food in China and most of the world. In its importance to consumers, it is second only to rice.
*millet: a member of the foxtail grass family, or its seeds, cultivated as a cereal, used as a stable food in ancient times, having been cultivated in China for more than 7,300 years, one of the earliest crops in the world.

和酸若苦，

陈吴羹些。

招魂

All paste and sauce now made,
Soup of Wu therein laid.

胹鳖炮羔，

有柘浆些。

Roast lamb and turtle stewed;
Sugarcane juice for food.

---

*lamb: a young sheep, especially one that is less than one year old or without permanent teeth.
*turtle: any of a large and widely distributed order of terrestrial or aquatic reptiles having a toothless beak and a soft body encased in a tough shell into which the head, tail and four legs may be withdrawn.
*sugarcane: *Saccharum officinarum*, perennial grass of the family *Poaceae*, primarily cultivated for its juice from which sugar is processed.

鹄酸臇凫,

煎鸿鸧些。

Mallard and swan beside,
Wild goose and dove pan-fried.

---

*mallard: a waterfowl like the duck, generally common and familiar within its extensive range. Males are distinctive with an iridescent green head, yellow bill, chestnut breast, and gray body. Females are mottled brown with orange and black splotches on the bill. Mallards are found anywhere with water, including city parks, backyard creeks, and various wetland habitats.
*swan: any of a largest waterfowl species of the subfamily *Anserinae*, family *Anatidae* (order *Anseriformes*), web-footed, long-necked, mostly pure white aquatic bird, allied to but heavier than the goose and noted for its grace on the water, as the whooper, the trumpeter swan, and the whistling swan.
*wild goose: an undomesticated goose that is caring and responsible, taken as a symbol of benevolence, righteousness, good manner, wisdom and faith in Chinese culture.
*dove: a pigeon, especially the mourning dove, turtledove, etc., a metaphor for one who takes a conciliatory attitude and advocates negotiations and compromise in contrast to the hawk, a symbol of one that always seeks military solutions.

324

露鸡臛蠵,

厉而不爽些。

招魂

Chicken braised, tortoise boiled,
The taste's so strong but it's not spoiled.

粔籹蜜饵,

有餦餭些。

Cookies, sweets, the whole lot;
And lo, maltose still hot.

瑶浆蜜勺,

实羽觞些。

Honey and brew so good,
Take your cup, try the food.

---

*chicken: a common gallinaceous farm bird, descended from various jungle fowl, especially the red jungle fowl, and developed in a number of breeds, raised for its flesh, eggs, and feathers.
*tortoise: a herbivorous reptile with a thick, hard shell that it can move its head and legs into for protection. It usually lives on land, moves very slowly, and sleeps during the winter, a symbol of longevity and felicity in Chinese culture.

挫糟冻饮,

酎清凉些。

Distilled wine cold like ice,
Cupfuls, cupfuls, so nice.

华酌既陈,

有琼浆些。

For the feast, tables laid;
Nectar wine finely made.

归来反故室,

敬而无妨些。

Do come back to our land direct;
It's all right, all stand with respect.

肴羞未通,

女乐罗些。

Not removed, dainties grand,
Girls come on with the band.

*nectar wine: a best quality wine likened to nectar. In Chinese mythology, nectar, also known as gold nectar, is an extract made by alchemists, for one who practised Wordism or the natural Wordist philosophy, wishing to become an immortal, and in Greek mythology, it is the drink of the gods or fairies.

招魂

陈钟按鼓,

造新歌些。

Bells set with a big drum,
New songs composed, come, come!

《涉江》《采菱》,

发《扬荷》些。

Wade O'er, *Pick Trapa*, trill!
One more song, *Sunny Hill*.

美人既醉,

朱颜酡些。

The belle's drunk, lo, her head,
Her complexion so red.

---

*Wade O'er: name of a Chu tune, otherwise known as *Crossing the River*.
*Pick Trapa: name of a Chu tune, also a common tune in the southern part of China.
*Sunny Hill: name of a Chu tune.

绘画：沈子琪

328

嬉光眇视,

目曾波些。

Her loving flirting glance,
Where a wave seems to dance.

被文服纤,

丽而不奇些。

She wears inwrought silk sheer,
Brilliant, so beautiful, but not queer.

长发曼鬋,

艳陆离些。

Her shining sable bun,
Brilliant, brilliant, well-done.

二八齐容,

起郑舞些。

Sixteen they are, they glance
And dance hot, Zheng-style dance.

招魂

衽若交竿，

抚案下些。

Their costumes swayed, tap, tap,
They bend down and they clap.

竽瑟狂会，

搷鸣鼓些。

Lute, flute, all played with zest,
Drums are beaten, pressed, pressed.

宫庭震惊，

发《激楚》些。

So moved, the court, the crowd;
Enhance is song aloud.

吴歈蔡讴，

奏大吕些。

Wu's melody, Cai's tune;
With Great Bell to commune.

---

*Enhance: a loud and strong tune of Chu.
*Wu: the State of Wu (12 Century B.C.-473 B.C.), in the lower reaches of the Long River, i.e., the Yangzi River, founded by King Civil's two elder uncles and annexed by the State of Yue, its neighboring state.
*Cai: the State of Cai (1046 B.C.-447 B.C.), a vassal state allotted to Cai, King Martial's younger brother, in today's Cai County, Henan Province, exterminated by Chu.
*Great Bell: name of a great bell in the Zhou dynasty and name of a melody, which sounds immense and magnificent.

330

士女杂坐，

乱而不分些。

招魂

Men and women sit there;
They sit singly, they make a pair.

放敶组缨，

班其相纷些。

Sashes, ribbons, untied,
All shine, all those supplied.

郑卫妖玩，

来杂陈些。

 From Zheng or Watch girls tall
Walk trippingly to th' hall.

---

*Watch: the State of Watch (1,115 B.C.-209 B.C.), Wei if transliterated, a fief allotted to Health Third (Kangshu), King Civil of Zhou's son, King Martial's younger brother, an important vassal state under Zhou's suzerainty, covering a large part of today's Shandong Province.

《激楚》之结,

独秀先些。

The ending of *Enhance*,
The best of all, perchance.

菎蔽象棋,

有六簙些。

Tools for ivory chess;
Six sticks played to progress.

分曹并进,

遒相迫些。

Each to the other goes,
Hard pressed, hard pressed, so close.

成枭而牟,

呼五白些。

招魂

Gained the fish, thrown the owl;
"Five white", they shout, they howl.

晋制犀比,

费白日些。

Chin's rhino hook does ray,
Thereby they end the day.

---

*Gained the fish, thrown the owl: fish and owl are names of chess-mates of a game called ivory chess played in ancient China.
*owl: a predatory nocturnal bird of prey, of the order *Strigiformes*, having large forward-directed eyes and head, short, sharply hooked bill, long powerful claws, and a circular facial disk of radiating feathers, regarded as ominous in Chinese culture.
*five white: gaining of five chess-mates by the white opponent playing an ivory chess game in ancient China.
*Jin: the State of Jin (1033 B.C.-376 B.C.), one of the most powerful vassal states under Suzerain Zhou, allotted to Yu, one of King Martial's princes and Great Grand's grandson. Jin, after a great dissension, was divided by its three ministers in 403 B.C. into three portions, that is, Way, Zhao and Han, each becoming an independent vassal state, hence the beginning of the epoch of Warring States.
*rhino: rhinoceros, any of a family of large, heavy, thick-skinned, plant-eating, perissodactylous mammals of tropical Africa and Asia, with one or two upright horns on the snout.

铿钟摇簴,

揳梓瑟些。

Bell and bell cot now sway;
Catalpa lutes they play.

娱酒不废,

沉日夜些。

They drink much, much they play,
Obsessed from night to day.

兰膏明烛,

华灯错些。

Orchid candles aglow;
Gorgeous lamps high and low.

结撰至思,

兰芳假些。

Think, think, poems they compose,
While fragrance o'er there flows.

---

*catalpa: any of a genus of hardy American and Asiatic trees of the begonia family, with large, heart-shaped leaves, showy clusters of trumpet-shaped flowers, and slender bean-like pods.

招魂

人有所极,

同心赋些。

Each with a gleeful heart;
For verse all play a part.

酎饮尽欢,

乐先故些。

Drink up, do drink up, please;
Make our fathers at ease.

魂兮归来!

反故居些。

O do come back, soul,
Come back to our land, whole.

乱曰:

The finale says,

献岁发春兮,

汩吾南征。

O new year, spring comes around,
In haste, I go, southbound.

菉蘋齐叶兮,

白芷生。

O small carp grass its leaves shows;
Angelica grows.

路贯庐江兮,

左长薄。

O along the Lodge, its bank,
Clusters grow so rank.

---

*small carp grass: *arthraxon hispidus*, an annual grass of wet areas, able to form dense stands, especially along shorelines, which can exclude native vegetation, native to Eastern Asia.
*angelica: any of a genus of odoriferous herbs of the carrot family, a Eurasian biennial or perennial whose roots and seeds yield a flavoring oil and whose young stems are often candied, a confection prepared from angelica.
*the Lodge: the Lodge River first mentioned in *Mountains and Seas*, unidentified now.

绘画：沈子琪

倚沼畦瀛兮,

遥望博。

O along the field, ahead,
The yonder plains spread.

青骊结驷兮,

齐千乘。

O a cart drawn by four steeds;
This cart all carts leads.

悬火延起兮,

玄颜烝。

O torches are on, so bright;
They light up the night.

步及骤处兮,

诱骋先。

O they come near, the carts stop;
Hunters run, tiptop!

抑骛若通兮,

引车右还。

O rein so held, front or rear;
They turn carts right, then veer.

与王趋梦兮,

课后先。

O with our lord, to Cloud Dream,
Who will best the team?

君王亲发兮,

惮青兕。

O our lord now draws the bow;
O shun the rhino, yo!

朱明承夜兮,

时不可以淹。

O after the night, it's light;
Non-stop, time is always in flight.

招魂

---

*Cloud Dream: alluding to the myth of Jade Girl and King Sow (King Xiang if transliterated). Jade Girl, Goddess of Mt. Witch, a beautiful fairy dwelling in Mt. Witch shaped herself as a cloud at dawn and turned into a rain at dusk. King Sow of Chu once met her in his dream, and had an intercourse overnight. The story was recorded by Jade Song, a student of Yuan Qu's, when he travelled to Cloud Dream Moor with King Sow.

*shun the rhino: According to Chu's folklore, one who has shot a rhino will die within three months.

皋兰被径兮,

斯路渐。

O orchids on the moor way,
The road's hid, oh, nay.

湛湛江水兮,

上有枫。

O the river is so blue,
Where maples grow.

目极千里兮,

伤春心。

O afar I turn my eyes;
Sad spring, all my sighs.

魂兮归来,

哀江南!

O do come back, soul;
South Land, great our dole!

---

*orchid: any of a large family (*Orchidaceae*, the orchid family) of perennial epiphytic or terrestrial monocotyledonous plants that usually have showy 3-petaled flowers with the middle petal enlarged into a lip and differing from the others in shape and color.

*maple: any of a large genus (*Acer*) (about 200 species) of deciduous trees or shrubs of the north temperate zone, but concentrated in China, with opposite leaves that turn red in autumn and a fruit of two joined samaras, a symbol of cordial love and good luck because of its bright fiery color.

渔父

The Fisherman

屈原既放，游于江潭，行吟泽畔，颜色憔悴，形容枯槁。

渔父见而问之曰："子非三闾大夫与？何故至于斯？"

屈原曰：

渔父

Yuan Qu, now exiled, wanders along the river, roving and chanting onto the marsh, so haggard and skinny. A fisherman. seeing him, asks: "Aren't you Lord of Three Portals, why reduced to such a state?" Yuan Qu replies,

---

*Yuan Qu: Yuan Qu (340 B.C.-278 B.C.), our poet of nobility, a loyal minister of Chu and a great patriot of China, who threw himself into the River Miluo, wronged by his king and other aristocrats and so aggrieved at his collapsing land. He is esteemed as the father of Chinese poetry by virtue of being the first named poet of importance and the author of the great and exceptionally long poem *Woebegone*. He is well-liked in China and East Asia. May Fifth of each year, known as Dragon Boat Festival, is the day when all Chinese and many East Asians like Koreans, Japanese, Vietnamese, Burmese, Malays and so on celebrate this poet, the greatest poet of all time.

*Lord of Three Portals: the title of a minister who holds a special position instituted in the State of Chu, mainly in charge of sacrificial rituals and education of the young of the three noble families of Chu, i.e. Zhao, Qu and Jing. Yuan Qu held this position before he was exiled.

"举世皆浊我独清,

众人皆醉我独醒,

是以见放。"

"I'm exiled because
All the world but me is sunken;
All the crowd but me is drunken."

渔父曰:

"圣人不凝滞于物,

而能与世推移。

世人皆浊,

何不淈其泥而扬其波?

众人皆醉,

何不餔其糟而歠其醨?

何故深思高举,

自令放为?"

The fisherman says,
"A saint's not stuck but changing with the world.
Since the world is sunken,
Why not roil the mud and splash the blue?
Since the crowd is drunken,
Why not eat the draff and drink the brew?
Why so profound and high flown that you've got exiled?"

渔父

屈原曰：

"吾闻之，

新沐者必弹冠，

新浴者必振衣；

安能以身之察察，

受物之汶汶者乎？

宁赴湘流，

葬于江鱼之腹中。

安能以皓皓之白，

而蒙世俗之尘埃乎？"

Yuan Qu replies, "I hear,
He who's newly bathed must pat his crown;
He who's newly washed must shake his gown.
Clean and clean, like pure crystal I remain;

---

*the Xiang: the Xiang River, one of the biggest rivers in today's Hunan Province, a branch of the Long River, a major source of Lake Cavehall, which is the second largest freshwater lake in China.
*bream: any of various freshwater cyprinoid fishes of the genus *Abramis*.

How can I with all that dirt myself stain?
I'd go to the Xiang stream
And be eaten up by a bream.
I should keep chaste and pure, and I must;
How can I drift away and breathe the dust?"

渔父莞尔而笑，鼓枻而去，歌曰：

The fisherman shows a thin smile and leaves, plying his oar while chanting:

"沧浪之水清兮，

可以濯吾缨；

沧浪之水浊兮，

可以濯吾足。"

"O the Blue's stream is limpid,
Wherewith I wash my sash;
O the Blue's stream is turbid,
Wherewith I wash my feet."

遂去，不复与言。

Thus leaves he, speaking no more.

---

*the Blue: the Blue River, which might be the Han River or its branch or the Summer River, both in today's Wuhan, one of the most prosperous river towns in China.

绘画：沈子琪

跋

Postscript

■ 我译屈原纯粹起于偶然——我译东西大都不是出于规划而是随缘。2019 年 4 月，有朋友邀请我去美国参加中美楚文化国际学术研讨会，为了写文章我便试译了《离骚》的前十几行。如下：

■ 离骚

帝高阳之苗裔兮，
朕皇考曰伯庸。
摄提贞于孟陬兮，
惟庚寅吾以降。
皇览揆余初度兮，
肇锡余以嘉名：
名余曰正则兮，
字余曰灵均。
纷吾既有此内美兮，
又重之以修能。
扈江离与辟芷兮，
纫秋兰以为佩。
汩余若将不及兮，
恐年岁之不吾与。

■ Woebegone

I'm a descendant from Lord High Sun,
O My late father called Medium First One.
In Prime Spring, Jupiter came to shine
O O'er my birth on Gilt Tiger, a month fine.
My sire observed the hour when came I
O And gave me beauteous names thereby:
My formal address was Rule Right,
O and my familiar one Pan Sprite.
With inner beauty I was so well blessed,
O and to raise my own worth I tried best.
A bulrush or balmy weed I don;
O an orchid-woven sash I put on.
The tide I can't catch up with runs fast;
O the time that does not wait for me flies past!

■ 这仅是一个尝试，但我觉得我的把握还是很到位的——诗人的身世与品格、中国的历法和礼制、诗歌的意象和韵律等应该说都得到了相应的表征。这时我才好奇地看看是否有人译过。结果发现了中外几个译本。我感到震惊：在这些译本中信息遗漏太多，误释太多，而且语篇不连贯，诗行之间无逻辑关系，自然也没有原作的气势和细腻，有的版本甚至不是诗体形式。楚地的文化身份、瑰丽浪漫的民族色彩，楚辞的美学特征竟然被译文遮蔽了。这实在对不起屈原,实在对不起中国文化了。

为了展示屈原的艺术成就和中华文化的神采,我感到有必要全译屈原。译屈原涉及对那个时代和区域特征的透彻理解,这需要花点时间。当时我注意力不在屈原,所以就没继续翻译。

当年10月,我带领几位同好与中国诗歌网联合创立《译典》栏目。中国诗歌研究院的莫真宝先生负责甄选原文。他选过四首屈原的诗,我随机译了。现不做更改,抄录如下:

■ 少司命

秋兰兮麋芜,
罗生兮堂下。
绿叶兮素华,
芳菲菲兮袭予。
夫人兮自有美子,
荪何以兮愁苦!
秋兰兮青青,
绿叶兮紫茎。
满堂兮美人,
忽独与余兮目成。
入不言兮出不辞,

乘回风兮载云旗。
悲莫悲兮生别离,
乐莫乐兮新相知。
荷衣兮蕙带,
儵而来兮忽而逝。
夕宿兮帝郊,
君谁须兮云之际?
与女沐兮咸池,
晞女发兮阳之阿。
望美人兮未来,
临风怳兮浩歌。
孔盖兮翠旍,
登九天兮抚彗星。
竦长剑兮拥幼艾,
荪独宜兮为民正。

■ The Young Priest

O Orchids and confervoides sprawl
In the yard in front of the hall.
O green leaves and blossoms wee,

The fragrance blows to assault me.
All have sons dear and daughters fair;
Why are you laden with care?
The orchids look so lush now;
In green leaves purple stalks bow.
The hall full of women sweet;
They turn their eyes and my eyes meet.
I come speechless and leave, not saying bye;
With a whirl, I hoist my flag to the sky.
Sad, I feel sadder when going apart;
Glad, I feel gladder new friendship to start.
I put on my clothes and sash,
I come in a rush and then away I dash.
I spend the night by God's Way;
For whom do you in clouds so long stay?
In Allpool I will wash my hair
And when the sun is up dry it in the air.
O the women sweet have not come along;
Before the wind I sing out a loud song.
Plumed hood large, feathered flag high,
You'll stroke a comet above in the sky.
A long sword you clasp, holding in your arms a child;

For the people you are just and mild.

山鬼

若有人兮山之阿,
被薜荔兮带女萝。
既含睇兮又宜笑,
子慕予兮善窈窕。
乘赤豹兮从文狸,
辛夷车兮结桂旗。
被石兰兮带杜衡,
折芳馨兮遗所思。
余处幽篁兮终不见天,
路险难兮独后来。
表独立兮山之上,
云容容兮而在下。
杳冥冥兮羌昼晦,
东风飘兮神灵雨。
留灵修兮憺忘归,
岁既晏兮孰华予?
采三秀兮於山间,

石磊磊兮葛蔓蔓。
怨公子兮怅忘归,
君思我兮不得闲。
山中人兮芳杜若,
饮石泉兮荫松柏,
君思我兮然疑作。
雷填填兮雨冥冥,
猨啾啾兮狖夜鸣。
风飒飒兮木萧萧,
思公子兮徒离忧。

Hill Ghost

One looms at the foot of the hill,
So I put on dodder and dill.
Beaming with love I start to smile;
My lithe figure can you beguile.
A red leopard I ride with a fox beside,
The cart of magnolia, a flag on the cassia.
A thoroughwort I don, wild ginger put on;
A blossom I pick, o for you I'm sick.
In the bamboo I cannot see the blue;

The road does wind, o I lag behind.
Upon the hill alone I stand;
The clouds roll on over the land.
It looks murky, much like the night;
With wind and rain spirits alight.
Waiting for Goddess, I forget the hour;
Times goes fast; why am I still a flower?
Ganoderma I pick in the dale;
Among the rocks kudzu spreads to prevail.
I grumble and forget to go back;
My Goddess, why don't come, alack?
Like life-flo, the one in hills is fine,
Who drinks of spring under the pine.
Do you miss me? My doubts entwine.
A thunder grumbles o a rain rumbles.
There monkeys trill o there langurs shrill;
There the wind soughs, o there the trees sough;
Thinking of you, o I'm annoyed now.

■ 国殇

操吴戈兮被犀甲,

车错毂兮短兵接。
旌蔽日兮敌若云,
矢交坠兮士争先。
凌余阵兮躐余行,
左骖殪兮右刃伤。
霾两轮兮絷四马,
援玉枹兮击鸣鼓。
天时怼兮威灵怒,
严杀尽兮弃原野。
出不入兮往不反,
平原忽兮路超远。
带长剑兮挟秦弓,
首虽离兮心不惩。
诚既勇兮又以武,
终刚强兮不可凌。
身既死兮神以灵,
魂魄毅兮为鬼雄。

■ The Death of the State

Rhino armor I wear, a spear I wave;

Hub to hub, the foe's knives and swords I brave.
The enemies like clouds, the flags shade the sun;
Arrows fall down and soldiers vie to run.
Our front invaded, our weapons clashed;
The leftist three steeds killed, the rightist slashed.
The two wheels trapped, the four steeds fall flat;
Drumsticks clasped fast, o the drum is thumped at.
It's all dark o, the ghost's with anger filled;
Deserted afield are those cruelly killed.
They've been off for long, o not back they are;
The plain is vast o the road rolls afar.
Carrying a sword long and a bow strong;
Head and trunk apart, o unchanged the heart.
O so brave and vigorous with might;
This great power o no enemy dare slight.
Though you've died, your spirit is never gone;
Of souls and ghosts, you are the bravest one.

■ 涉江

余幼好此奇服兮，
年既老而不衰。

带长铗之陆离兮,
冠切云之崔嵬。
被明月兮佩宝璐。
世混浊而莫余知兮,
吾方高驰而不顾。
驾青虬兮骖白螭,
吾与重华游兮瑶之圃。
登昆仑兮食玉英,
与天地兮同寿,
与日月兮同光。
哀南夷之莫吾知兮,
旦余济乎江湘。
乘鄂渚而反顾兮,
欸秋冬之绪风。
步余马兮山皋,
邸余车兮方林。
乘舲船余上沅兮,
齐吴榜以击汰。
船容与而不进兮,
淹回水而疑滞。
朝发枉陼兮,

夕宿辰阳。
苟余心其端直兮,
虽僻远之何伤。
入溆浦余儃佪兮,
迷不知吾所如。
深林杳以冥冥兮,
乃猿狖之所居。
山峻高以蔽日兮,
下幽晦以多雨。
霰雪纷其无垠兮,
云霏霏而承宇。
哀吾生之无乐兮,
幽独处乎山中。
吾不能变心而从俗兮,
固将愁苦而终穷。
接舆髡首兮,
桑扈臝行。
忠不必用兮,
贤不必以。
伍子逢殃兮,
比干菹醢。

与前世而皆然兮,
吾又何怨乎今之人!
余将董道而不豫兮,
固将重昏而终身!
乱曰:
鸾鸟凤皇,日以远兮。
燕雀乌鹊,巢堂坛兮。
露申辛夷,死林薄兮。
腥臊并御,芳不得薄兮。
阴阳易位,时不当兮。
怀信侘傺,
忽乎吾将行兮!

■ Crossing the River

I've loved strange clothes since I was a child;
Now I'm old, I remain so styled.
I wear a long sword on my waist,
And don a crown so highly raised,
And carry a jade disc brightly chaste.
The world dark, none knows how I aspire;

I just go ahead, my head raised higher.
A dragon blue aided by dragons white
Is what I'll ride with Chunghua to tour a godly sight.
Mt. Queen I'll climb and on nectar I'll dine,
So I'll live long like Heaven and earth,
And with the sun and the moon I'll shine.
How sad, no southerners do me understand!
Tomorrow, I'll row to an alien land.
I come ashore at the E and look back;
The chill wintry wind blows, alack.
Up a hill my horse I lead and drive;
In my cart at a square wood I arrive.
Sitting in a boat, upstream I go;
The boatmen try their best to row.
So slow, the boat can't go ahead;
In whirlpools it pauses instead.
In the morn Wangzhu I leave
And sleep at Chenyang at eve.
So long as I'm upright and square,
However far off I don't care.
In Xupu I hesitate, oh no;
So lost, I don't know where to go.

Dark and deep the wood and the dell,
It's where monkeys and langurs dwell.
The mountains rise to shade the sun;
It's dark below, it's raining on.
It's all snow, flying without bound;
The roof is with clouds crowned.
I deplore my life without glee;
My solitude the hills see.
I can't yield to the world, I shan't change my will,
So I'm unrequited, poor and ill.
Jieyu had his hair cut off;
Sanghu, naked, did all doff.
A loyal one is not used,
A sage one is refused!
O Wu Zixu was erased,
Bigan was cut into paste.
It's the same now as before;
Why should I today's world deplore?
Without hesitation, I'll keep my way,
Though in darkness for life I'll stay.
The lay is like this:
Phoenixes, swans, o away you all fly;

Sparrows, magpies, o you nest in halls high.
Daphne, magnolia, in wild woods they die;
Urine and dung so mixed , balm can't get nearby.
Upside down day and night,
It's a wrong time, not right.
Loyal but unused, I grieve;
For a better place I now leave.

■ 也许我工作太忙,也许我同时也在译其他典籍,比如《李太白全集》《孝经》,还有《译典》每个工作日推送的诗歌,这几首译完之后我就忘了。我真的全忘了!

2021年11月8日朱焱炜老师向我要李白、杜甫、白居易的一些译诗,还问我有没有译过屈原的《橘颂》和陶渊明的《桃花源记》。唐朝这几位诗人的诗歌我都译过,可是《橘颂》和《桃花源记》我好像没译过。我不想让她失望,于是就译了。我想,既然译了屈原的《橘颂》,以前还译过十几行《离骚》,那我干脆把屈原的诗都译了吧。于是,搁下手头正校对的《杜甫诗歌全集英译》,一发不可收拾,埋头十天,译完了屈原的楚辞。后来我才发现2019年11月译过以上四首。刘勰说:变文之数无方。大家一定很好奇:出自同一译者的不同时段的版本是否有差别。当然,这是不同场景下造就的不同的译本。措辞不同、韵脚不同,但又都是屈原的精神和风格。

语言太神奇了,翻译太神奇了!

以上这几首译文算是一气呵成的，译完后我也没再核查。为了保留原貌，现在也不做修改。

　　朱老师的请求触发了我对屈原的感觉，于是我便沉下心来着手翻译了。我感到一下子就进入了屈原的世界。我似乎不是在翻译而是感受他的心路历程，而英语的诗行也似乎是发自他内心的自然流动。为此契合，我激动不已。

　　译者要对作者、读者负责，不可过于相信自己的感觉，不可放飞自己的浪漫。他必须严肃而客观地对待译文。于是译文草成之后我便精心地打磨了。我一个音节一个音节地核对诗行，还请了丁后银先生一个音节一个音节地核对，同时又请了古文专家莫真宝先生核对文字。经莫先生提议，我买了《楚辞植物图鉴》，一一比对诗中出现的植物，并找到对应的英文，最后又斟酌诗的意义，核查人名、地名并深研典故，以免信息有所遗漏和偏差。

　　精益求精要求我们：如果有一个词素可以精进，那也毫不犹豫。比如"胹鳖炮羔，有柘浆些"我初译为"Roast lamb and turtle stewed; Syrup to go with food.""柘浆"译为"syrup"，不算错吧，而且也满足了诗体的要求，但语义上并不准确。查考得知"柘"即"诸柘"，即"甘蔗"。这说明在战国时期的楚地已经栽培甘蔗了，这一信息应该传达。为此，我将后一行调整为"Sugarcane juice for food"。再如，"既替余以蕙纕兮"中的"蕙"译作"basil""orchid""tonka bean""coumarou""lavender"都不能算错，我先译作"orchid"，但感觉"orchid"不属于香草，古人不一定会佩戴，"basil"更好些。对照《楚辞植物图鉴》，果然是"basil"，于是便做了调整。这个更能代表屈原，我放心了。

有时斟酌也会有反复，比如"菉蕬"是"荩草"，拉丁语名称是"Arthraxon hispidus"，但此处的翻译不能用，语体不对，音节也太多，必须找到英语对等的名称。我先找到"small carp grass"，后来我又查证，改为"clover fern"，再后来又比照图片，再改回"small carp grass"。《离骚》中有28种植物，都一一核对。最麻烦的问题是词汇空缺，即目的语中没有对等成分。《离骚》中有些植物英文中没有对应的成分，如"宿莽"，还有的植物外国根本就没有，现在中国也没有了，比如"揭车"，但这也不能不译。我不愿采用实为不译的音译法，所以便查找资料根据所描述的特征造词，前者我译为"lodging-grass"，后者译为"auragrass"。

精准是翻译的终极追求，译者要尽可能逼近原作。比如"流澌纷兮将来下"我初译为"I will follow you close o with the tide"，经查证，"流澌"含有"冰"的成分，于是将"the tide"改为"floe tide"。再如"伯林雉经"是以申生自缢叙说商纣王自焚，我初译为"Chow burned himself on fire"。查考得知"雉经"是"上吊自杀"，遂改为"Chow hanged himself on fire"，如此"自焚"和"自缢"都包含了。有的词要在语境中判断，比如"玄蜂若壶些"中的"玄蜂"孤立地看可以译为"black bee"，但根据前后关系却应译为"black wasp"。翻译中常有文字陷阱，译者难免望文生义，如"石濑兮浅浅"。"浅浅"很容易理解为"shallow""flat"，但下一行是"飞龙兮翩翩"——龙船快行如飞。如果河很浅，那么船如何飞行呢？核查时发现其读音是 jianjian 而非 qianqian，意思是"水流迅激"，所以译文就从"flat"改为"swift"了。

总之，对于字词我不敢有丝毫的懈怠，因为我深知精准就是经典翻译的生命。

字词的精确是翻译质量的保障，但这并不是诗的保障。屈原楚辞的译文必须是诗。译文必须在诗体特征和音步上还原屈原的独到之处。散体不符合屈原的设计，也不符合读者的预期。

诗，当然要有诗的形式，格律诗尤其要有韵律——这一点是绝对不能含混的。对于格律诗的翻译我做了类比性的设定：三言类比为五音节即两音步；四言类比为六音节即三音步；五言类比为八音节即四音步；六言类比为九音节即四音步或五音步；七言类比为十音节即五音步；八言类比为十二音节即六音步；九言类比为十四音节即七音步。韵式多类比为 aabb, abab。这样的设定会限制译者的自由吧？

在限制中自由翱翔则更显风姿。

楚辞不是严格的格律诗，多为长短句，其中多夹杂兮、也、其等语气词或叹词，具有浓郁的地方色彩。具有凸显意义的"兮"我以"O"类比，为一对一的对等，其他则采用我一贯的做法，即七言类比为五音步或 10 个音节等，不一而足。以此可以表现屈原的语气和抑扬顿挫。

这是基本格局,其目的是能够全面地代表屈原。

每一丁点的改进都是非凡的跨越。

让我们逼近完美,让我们伟大的诗人在世界文学的宝库中永生。

Postscript

I translated Yuan Qu all by accident. I'm seldom scheduled to translate anything but spurred by chance. In April, 2019, I was invited by a friend to attend a Sino-American symposium on Chu Culture in U.S.A. For a paper to deliver, I tried translating a dozen lines of *Woebegone* (*Li-sao*), as follows:

■ 离骚

帝高阳之苗裔兮,

朕皇考曰伯庸。

摄提贞于孟陬兮,

惟庚寅吾以降。

皇览揆余初度兮,

肇锡余以嘉名:

名余曰正则兮,

字余曰灵均。

纷吾既有此内美兮,

又重之以修能。

扈江离与辟芷兮，
纫秋兰以为佩。
汨余若将不及兮，
恐年岁之不吾与。

Woebegone

I'm a descendant from Lord High Sun,
O My late father called Medium First One.
In Prime Spring, Jupiter came to shine
O O'er my birth on Gilt Tiger, a month fine.
My sire observed the hour when came I
O And gave me beauteous names thereby:
My formal address was Rule Right,
O and my familiar one Pan Sprite.
With inner beauty I was so well blessed,
O and to raise my own worth I tried best.
A bulrush or balmy weed I don;
O an orchid-woven sash I put on.
The tide I can't catch up with runs fast;
O the time that does not wait for me flies past!

■ I thought it a rather exact rendering, though it was a mere try . The poet's saga and character, Chinese calendar and rituals, poetic imagery and prosody, I suppose, were appropriately represented. Now I felt curious if anybody else had translated it and I found a few versions by Chinese and foreigners. I felt surprised with the losses and errors in these versions, too many of them. Besides, the texts are not coherent, without logic relations or any trace of the momentum or finesse of the original, and some are not even metrical. The cultural identity of Chu, the romantic splendor of the nation, the aesthetic features of Chu lyrics are all eclipsed by translation. This falls short of Yuan Qu, and falls short of Chinese culture.

To reveal Yuan Qu's artistic achievements and the charm of Chinese culture, I thought it necessary to translate all of his poems. This involves a good understanding of the era and provincial features, and it takes time. As my attention was not focused on Yuan Qu then, I dropped it.

In October the same year, I initiated Translating Classics on Chinese Poetry Net with a few friends. I translated four of Yuan Qu's poems once chosen by Mr. Zhenbao Mo from Poetry Institution of China, an editor in charge of selecting originals. Now I copy them below without any change:

■ 少司命

秋兰兮麋芜,
罗生兮堂下;
绿叶兮素华,
芳菲菲兮袭予;
夫人兮自有美子,
荪何以兮愁苦。
秋兰兮青青,
绿叶兮紫茎;
满堂兮美人
忽独与余兮目成;
入不言兮出不辞,
乘回风兮载云旗。
悲莫悲兮生别离,
乐莫乐兮新相知;
荷衣兮蕙带,

儵而来兮忽而逝；
夕宿兮帝郊，
君谁须兮云之际。
与女沐兮咸池，
晞女发兮阳之阿；
望美人兮未来，
临风怳兮浩歌。
孔盖兮翠旍，
登九天兮抚彗星；
竦长剑兮拥幼艾，
荪独宜兮为民正。

The Young Priest

O Orchids and confervoides sprawl
In the yard in front of the hall.
O green leaves and blossoms wee,
The fragrance blows to assault me.
All have sons dear and daughters fair;

Why are you laden with care?
The orchids look so lush now;
In green leaves purple stalks bow.
The hall full of women sweet;
They turn their eyes and my eyes meet.
I come speechless and leave, not saying bye;
With a whirl, I hoist my flag to the sky.
Sad, I feel sadder when going apart;
Glad, I feel gladder new friendship to start.
I put on my clothes and sash,
I come in a rush and then away I dash.
I spend the night by God's Way;
For whom do you in clouds so long stay?
In Allpool I will wash my hair
And when the sun is up dry it in the air.
O the women sweet have not come along;
Before the wind I sing out a loud song.
Plumed hood large, feathered flag high,
You'll stroke a comet above in the sky.
A long sword you clasp, holding in your arms a child;
For the people you are just and mild.

山鬼

若有人兮山之阿！
被薜荔兮带女萝。
既含睇兮又宜笑,
子慕予兮善窈窕。
乘赤豹兮从文狸,
辛夷车兮结桂旗。
被石兰兮带杜衡,
折芳馨兮遗所思。
余处幽篁兮终不见天,
路险难兮独后来。
表独立兮山之上,
云容容兮而在下。
杳冥冥兮羌昼晦,
东风飘兮神灵雨。
留灵修兮憺忘归,

岁既晏兮孰华予?
采三秀兮於山间,
石磊磊兮葛蔓蔓。
怨公子兮怅忘归,
君思我兮不得闲。
山中人兮芳杜若,
饮石泉兮荫松柏。
君思我兮然疑作。
雷填填兮雨冥冥,
猨啾啾兮狖夜鸣。
风飒飒兮木萧萧,
思公子兮徒离忧。

■ Hill Ghost

One looms at the foot of the hill,
So I put on dodder and dill.
Beaming with love I start to smile;

My lithe figure can you beguile.
A red leopard I ride with a fox beside,
The cart of magnolia, a flag on the cassia.
A thoroughwort I don, wild ginger put on;
A blossom I pick, o for you I'm sick.
In the bamboo I cannot see the blue;
The road does wind, o I lag behind.
Upon the hill alone I stand;
The clouds roll on over the land.
It looks murky, much like the night;
With wind and rain spirits alight.
Waiting for Goddess, I forget the hour;
Times goes fast; why am I still a flower?
Ganoderma I pick in the dale;
Among the rocks kudzu spreads to prevail.
I grumble and forget to go back;
My Goddess, why don't come, alack?
Like life-flo, the one in hills is fine,
Who drinks of spring under the pine.
Do you miss me? My doubts entwine.
A thunder grumbles o a rain rumbles.
There monkeys trill o there langurs shrill;

There the wind soughs, o there the trees sough;
Thinking of you, o I'm annoyed now.

■ 国殇

操吴戈兮被犀甲,
车错毂兮短兵接。
旌蔽日兮敌若云,
矢交坠兮士争先。
凌余阵兮躐余行,
左骖殪兮右刃伤。
霾两轮兮絷四马,
援玉枹兮击鸣鼓。
天时怼兮威灵怒,
严杀尽兮弃原野。
出不入兮往不反,
平原忽兮路超远。
带长剑兮挟秦弓,

首虽离兮心不惩。

诚既勇兮又以武,

终刚强兮不可凌。

身既死兮神以灵,

魂魄毅兮为鬼雄。

■ The Death of the State

Rhino armor I wear, a spear I wave;
Hub to hub, the foe's knives and swords I brave.
The enemies like clouds, the flags shade the sun;
Arrows fall down and soldiers vie to run.
Our front invaded, our weapons clashed;
The leftist three steeds killed, the rightist slashed.
The two wheels trapped, the four steeds fall flat;
Drumsticks clasped fast, o the drum is thumped at.
It's all dark o, the ghost's with anger filled;
Deserted afield are those cruelly killed.
They've been off for long, o not back they are;
The plain is vast o the road rolls afar.

Carrying a sword long and a bow strong;
Head and trunk apart, o unchanged the heart.
O so brave and vigorous with might;
This great power o no enemy dare slight.
Though you've died, your spirit is never gone;
Of souls and ghosts, you are the bravest one.

■ 涉江

余幼好此奇服兮,

年既老而不衰。

带长铗之陆离兮,

冠切云之崔嵬。

被明月兮佩宝璐。

世混浊而莫余知兮,

吾方高驰而不顾。

驾青虬兮骖白螭,

吾与重华游兮瑶之圃。

登昆仑兮食玉英,

与天地兮同寿,
与日月兮同光。
哀南夷之莫吾知兮,
旦余济乎江湘。
乘鄂渚而反顾兮,
欸秋冬之绪风。
步余马兮山皋,
邸余车兮方林。
乘舲船余上沅兮,
齐吴榜以击汰。
船容与而不进兮,
淹回水而疑滞。
朝发枉陼兮,
夕宿辰阳。
苟余心其端直兮,
虽僻远之何伤。
入溆浦余儃徊兮,

迷不知吾所如。
深林杳以冥冥兮，
乃猿狖之所居。
山峻高以蔽日兮，
下幽晦以多雨。
霰雪纷其无垠兮，
云霏霏而承宇。
哀吾生之无乐兮，
幽独处乎山中。
吾不能变心而从俗兮，
固将愁苦而终穷。
接舆髡首兮，
桑扈臝行。
忠不必用兮，
贤不必以。
伍子逢殃兮，
比干菹醢。

与前世而皆然兮，

吾又何怨乎今之人！

余将董道而不豫兮，

固将重昏而终身！

乱曰：

鸾鸟凤皇，日以远兮。

燕雀乌鹊，巢堂坛兮。

露申辛夷，死林薄兮。

腥臊并御，芳不得薄兮。

阴阳易位，时不当兮。

怀信侘傺，

忽乎吾将行兮！

Crossing the River

I've loved strange clothes since I was a child;
Now I'm old, I remain so styled.
I wear a long sword on my waist,

And don a crown so highly raised,
And carry a jade disc brightly chaste.
The world dark, none knows how I aspire;
I just go ahead, my head raised higher.
A dragon blue aided by dragons white
Is what I'll ride with Chunghua to tour a godly sight.
Mt. Queen I'll climb and on nectar I'll dine,
So I'll live long like Heaven and earth,
And with the sun and the moon I'll shine.
How sad, no southerners do me understand!
Tomorrow, I'll row to an alien land.
I come ashore at the E and look back;
The chill wintry wind blows, alack.
Up a hill my horse I lead and drive;
In my cart at a square wood I arrive.
Sitting in a boat, upstream I go;
The boatmen try their best to row.
So slow, the boat can't go ahead;
In whirlpools it pauses instead.
In the morn Wangzhu I leave
And sleep at Chenyang at eve.
So long as I'm upright and square,

However far off I don't care.
In Xupu I hesitate, oh no;
So lost, I don't know where to go.
Dark and deep the wood and the dell,
It's where monkeys and langurs dwell.
The mountains rise to shade the sun;
It's dark below, it's raining on.
It's all snow, flying without bound;
The roof is with clouds crowned.
I deplore my life without glee;
My solitude the hills see.
I can't yield to the world, I shan't change my will,
So I'm unrequited, poor and ill.
Jieyu had his hair cut off;
Sanghu, naked, did all doff.
A loyal one is not used,
A sage one is refused!
O Wu Zixu was erased,
Bigan was cut into paste.
It's the same now as before;
Why should I today's world deplore?
Without hesitation, I'll keep my way,

Though in darkness for life I'll stay.
The lay is like this:
Phoenixes, swans, o away you all fly;
Sparrows, magpies, o you nest in halls high.
Daphne, magnolia, in wild woods they die;
Urine and dung so mixed, balm can't get nearby.
Upside down day and night,
It's a wrong time, not right.
Loyal but unused, I grieve;
For a better place I now leave.

■ Probably because I was so busy or because I was translating other classics like *Pai Li's Complete Works*, *Filial Piety* and poems to be released each working day for the column Translating Classics, I forgot having ever translated these poems. I forgot them all.

■ On November 8, 2021, Miss Yanwei Zhu, who would ask me of some translations of Bai Li, Fu Du and Juyi Bai, asked if I had translated Yuan Qu's *Ode to the Orange* and Yuanming Tao's *Peach Blossom Source*. I had translated these Tang poets but not the other two. I took to translating them lest I should disappoint her. As I mused, since I had translated Yuan Qu's *Ode to the Orange* and a dozen lines of his *Woebegone*, why not translate them all? It never rains but pours! Laying aside *A Complete Edition of Fu Tu's Poems in Chinese and English*, which I was proofreading, I, burying myself for 10 days, finished Yuan Qu's poetry in a breath. Only now did I find the four translations done in November, 2019. I forgot them completely. As Xie Liu asserted, "Language has unlimited variations". One may be curious whether the translations done by the same translator at different times may differ. Of course, they are different versions done under different circumstances. Despite the different wordings and different rhymes, the poet's spirit and style remain the same.

- ■ Language is a miracle and translation is a miracle too!
- ■ These several translations were done at a dash and I have not glanced back to check them. I let them be even now, with no improvements ever tried.
- ■ Miss Zhu's request triggered my feeling for Yuan Qu, so I settled down to translate him. I seemed to have entered Yuan Qu's world all at once, not doing the translation but feeling what he was feeling, and my English lines seemed to be a spontaneous flow from his heart. With such a concordance, I was so excited.
- ■ A translator should be responsible to the author and the reader. He should not be too confident with what he feels, and he should not let his romance fly. He must be serious and objective with his translation. So the translations in this collection I have honed with great care. I checked the lines syllable by syllable and I asked Mr. Houyin Ding to have a syllable-by-syllable check. At the same time, I asked Mr. Zhenbao Mo, a scholar of classics, to examine the original, and upon his suggestion I bought a copy of *Pictures of Plants in Chu Lyrics* to correlate plants appearing in the poems with their English counterparts. And of course, I weighed over the semantics and checked names of people and places and delved into the

allusions in case of lapses and inadequacies.

■   The pursuit for perfection requires a translator to approximate the original without any hesitation. He does not give in even if a morpheme may be improved. Take "胹鳖炮羔，有柘浆些" for example. My first rendering was "Roast lamb and turtle stewed; Syrup to go with food". The word "syrup" for "柘浆" is no mistake and it fits in well with the meter, but it's not so exact semantically, because "柘", a short term for "诸柘", means "sugarcane". This tells us the cultivation of sugarcane began at least as early as the Warring States period, as should be expressed, so I changed the line into "Sugarcane juice for food". For another example, the "蕙" in "既替余以蕙纕兮" can be interpreted as "basil" "orchid" "tonka bean" "coumarou" or "lavender", and my first translation was "orchid", about which I doubted, because orchids are not a fragrant herb, which ancients might not wear. Might "basil" be a better choice? Checking *Pictures of Plants of Chu Lyrics*, I found the word "basil" going with the picture, so I made a change, feeling reassured it is closer to the author.

■   Sometimes, one need ruminate over the diction, for example," 蓑蘋" is also called "荩草", "*Arthraxon hispidus*" in Latin, but it was not proper to be used in the translation because of the tenor and the number of syllables, so an equivalent English word is necessary. I found "small carp grass" and, after weighing, changed it into "clover fern", and finally came back to "small carp grass" after checking the picture book. Altogether, Yuan Qu used 28 plants in *Woebegone*, which I checked one by one. A big challenge is what we call lexical gap, that is, one cannot always find an equivalent. Some plants have no English names, like "宿莽", and some plants are non-existent in countries other than China and not existent even in China now, "揭车" for example. But you should not skip it. As I don't like transliteration that is actually non-translation, what I did was to coin a word based on the features described. For the former, I coined "lodging-grass", and for the latter "auragrass".

■ Exactitude is a translator's ultimate pursuit. He should try his best to approximate the original. For example, I first translated "流澌纷兮将来下" into "I will follow you close o with the tide". A consultation of a dictionary found "ice" in the tide, so I changed it into "floe tide". For another example, "伯林雉经" alluding to Outbirth's suicide by hanging himself, tells of King Chow's burning of himself. As "雉经" suggests "hanging oneself" according to an annotation, "Chow burned himself on fire" was changed into "Chow hanged himself on fire", including both "hanging himself" and "burning himself". Some words need to be judged in context, for example, 玄蜂 in "玄蜂若壶些" can be "black bee" out of context, but in context, "black wasp" is more appropriate. And there are often traps that may cause a translator to fall into. For example, "浅浅" in "石濑兮浅浅" may mislead one to the meaning of "shallow" or "flat", but the next line is "飞龙兮翩翩", meaning "the boat rows so fast as if to fly". If a river or stream is shallow, how can the boat run like flying? As found in research, the pronunciation is jianjian instead of qianqian, meaning "flowing rapidly", so "flat" was changed into "swift".

■ All in all, I dare not be slack with any single word, because I know exactitude is the life of the translation of a classic.

■ The exactitude of words is a guarantee of the quality of translation but it is not a guarantee of a poem. The translations of Yuan Qu's poems must be poems in their own right; they must be a facsimile of the poet's idiosyncrasy. Prose does not accord with Yuan Qu's design nor with a reader's expectation.

■ A poem, of course, must have a poetic form, especially meter and rhyme in the case of metric poetry, as one should never ever neglect. As for the translation of metric poetry, I have made an analogical design of meter and rhyme, for example, a three-character line is rendered into five syllables or dimeter, a four-character line is rendered into six syllables or trimeter, a five-character line into eight syllables or a tetrameter, a seven-character line into ten syllables or pentameter, an eight-character line into twelve syllables or hexameter, a nine-character line into fourteen syllables or heptameter, and in terms of rhyme or rhyming scheme, running rhyme (aabb), alternating rhyme (abab) or ballad quatrain is generally adopted by analogy. Does such a postulation constrain a translator's freedom?

■ A free soar within constraints displays greater charms.

■ Chu lyrics are not regular metric poetry, radiant with indigenous features and often alternating with long and short lines, interspersed with exclamatory particles, like " 兮 " or " 也 ", radiant with provincialism and vernacularism. In the case of the salient " 兮 ", I adopt "o" by analogy for exact correspondence, and in terms of poetic lines, I adopt meters like pentameter or 10-syllable lines and so on so as to represent Yuan Qu's tone and cadence. These are basic templates for the whole representation of Yuan Qu's poems.

■ A tiny bit of improvement is a great leap forward.

■ Let's get closer to perfection to immortalize our great author in the thesaurus of world literature.

图书在版编目（CIP）数据

屈原楚辞英译 / 赵彦春译、注. -- 上海：上海大学出版社，2023.1
ISBN 978-7-5671-4541-2

Ⅰ. ①屈… Ⅱ. ①赵… Ⅲ. ①楚辞－译文－英文 Ⅳ. ①I222.3

中国版本图书馆 CIP 数据核字 (2022) 第 230699 号

责任编辑	徐雁华
助理编辑	于　欣
书籍设计	张天志　缪炎栩
技术编辑	金　鑫　钱宇坤

屈原楚辞英译

赵彦春 译·注

出版发行	上海大学出版社出版发行
地　　址	上海市上大路 99 号
邮政编码	200444
网　　址	www.shupress.cn
发行热线	021-66135109
出 版 人	戴骏豪

印　　刷	上海颛辉印刷厂有限公司
经　　销	各地新华书店
开　　本	787 mm×1092 mm　1/16
印　　张	25.25
字　　数	505 千
版　　次	2023 年 1 月第 1 版
印　　次	2023 年 1 月第 1 次
书　　号	ISBN 978-7-5671-4541-2/I.666
定　　价	188.00 元

版权所有　侵权必究
如发现本书有印装质量问题请与印刷厂质量科联系
联系电话：021-57602918